Th

She started cycling slowly towards the gates and for a few minutes I simply watched her go . The thing was, I knew she was scared too. She didn't want to go into that garden any more than I did but she was forcing herself. It made me ashamed of myself.

'Wait a minute,' I called after her, my voice rather shaky. 'I've changed my mind.'

Although Laura was smiling at me, I thought I was probably making a mistake. What I didn't know then was that I was doing the silliest thing I'd ever done in my life.

The Creepy Tale

Ritchie Perry

RED FOX

A Red Fox Book
Published by Arrow Books Limited
20 Vauxhall Bridge Road, London SW1V 2SA

An imprint of the Random Century Group

London Melbourne Sydney Auckland
Johannesburg and agencies throughout
the world

First published by Hutchinson Children's Books 1989
Red Fox edition 1990

Text © Ritchie Perry 1989

Printed and bound in Great Britain by
Courier International Ltd, Tiptree, Essex

ISBN 0 09 966890 4

1

Although there was a twig stuck up my right nostril and some thorns hooked into the seat of my jeans, I didn't dare move. Dad was looking my way and he had the hose-pipe in his hand. It definitely wasn't part of the master plan for me to get soaking wet. He and the neighbour's cat have been sworn enemies ever since they had their competition to see whether Dad could plant bulbs faster than the cat dug them up. If he thought it was Tiddles in the shrubbery, I was going to get drenched. Mind you, I was surprised Dad had heard me because a lot of the time he seems to be stone deaf. Mum can shout as loud as she likes about helping with the washing-up or cleaning the car or going to the shops and he never hears a word. I'd brushed against a branch halfway across the garden and he'd swung round immediately. It was amazing.

After a moment or two Dad went back to watering the geraniums or whatever and I pulled the twig out of my nose. The thorns were more of a problem, lying the way I was. Although I managed to work them free without too much damage to the treasured Venables backside, there was a nasty ripping sound as they came loose from my jeans. I'd have to tell Mum I'd been savaged by the Alsatian round the corner. On second thoughts, I decided it might be easier to tell the truth. The poor dog was so ancient it had lost most of its teeth. I could hardly tell Mum the holes had been caused by a vicious suck.

Not for the first time, I wondered why I was the one in the shrubbery. After all, this was all Laura's bright idea; she was the one who wanted to get her own back on Dad. It had all started when Laura entered this story-writing contest in the *Wroxford Gazette*. As soon as he found out, Dad rang her up from work, disguising his voice and pretending to be a reporter. It was almost ten minutes before Laura had cottoned on to who it was and realized she hadn't really won a prize for £10. Now Laura was paying him back, which meant she should have been the one risking life, limb and backside in the middle of the jungle Dad called a shrubbery. This was the way it always went, though. Laura was the one who had the bright ideas and I was the poor idiot who did all the hard work. My trouble is I'm too nice. I'm always prepared to do other people a favour. Or perhaps I really am an idiot, after all.

I was just about to start crawling forward again when I discovered I had company. Normally I quite like cats but I agree with Dad about Tiddles. It is big and fat and ginger, which makes the beast look pretty terrible, and it smells far worse. I don't know whether the Hendersons feed Tiddles on baked beans or whether it is something else, but Tiddles is an insult to noses. Dad said that if we ever went to war the RAF only had to drop Tiddles on Moscow and the Russians would be gassed into surrender. I thought it was a shame the RAF couldn't do a few practice runs now. Tiddles had crept up on me and was purring like a maniac while it rubbed its nose against mine. It made me realize how lucky I'd been when I'd only had to bother about twigs and thorns.

'Go away,' I hissed. 'Scat.'

Tiddles just purred some more and walked round to sit on my back. This was really terrific. I mean, I definitely didn't need half a ton of stinking cat on my back when I was trying to crawl without making any noise. On the other hand, I didn't have much choice. The stupid creature had always liked me and I knew I wouldn't get rid of it easily. Fortunately, there wasn't much further to go. Another metre or so and I could see Laura as well as Dad. She was sitting round the corner of the house, out of sight of Dad, and she had the hose-pipe running across her knees. A quick check to make sure Dad was still busy with the geraniums, then I gave Laura the thumbs-up sign. She flashed her teeth in a smile before she bent the length of hose over and held it tightly. It took Dad a moment to realize the water wasn't coming through any longer. Then he did what he always did in moments of crisis: shouted for Mum.

'Mary,' he bellowed. 'Mary.'

'What is it, dear?'

Mum was using her special voice, the one she saved for mental defectives, us kids and Dad when he was in one of his moods.

'It's nothing really, my sweet.' Dad had a great line in sarcasm. 'It's just that I find it awfully difficult to water the border when the tap is turned off.'

'I would too, dear. That's why I always turn the water on before I go into the garden.'

'So do I, beloved.' Dad's voice was back at a bellow and his face was turning red. 'The hose was working fine until some idiot turned the tap off.'

'Well I certainly haven't touched it.'

'Oh.'

This took Dad by surprise. When anything goes

3

wrong, he always assumes it is Mum's fault unless Laura and I are there to blame. For a second or two he examined the hose but no water came through, even when he gave it a shake. It wasn't likely to while Laura was bending it in knots.

'Is the connection all right?'

'It looks fine to me, dear.'

I could see Mum at the kitchen window, looking down at Laura. It hadn't taken her long to work out what was going on but she wasn't about to blow the whistle on us.

'Oh,' Dad said again.

I'd told Laura it wasn't going to work. I'd said it was only in comedy films that people actually looked down the end of hoses, but I was wrong as usual. Dad even lifted it right up to his face and closed one eye so he could see better.

'Please let him keep it there,' I whispered to myself as I waved my hand up and down.

He did. Laura had let go of the hose and a moment later Dad had all the water he could ever want. It was beautiful to watch. Mum must have turned the tap full on once she realized what was going down and the water came out in a great jet, knocking Dad's silly yachting cap clean off his head. He was soaked and I was hurting all over. It was really painful laughing as much as I was without making a sound. Not that I laughed for long. Dad wasn't too wet to forget the noise he'd heard in the shrubbery.

'All right, you little monster,' he said, advancing across the lawn towards my hiding place. 'Let's see how you like a taste of your own medicine.'

This was something Laura must have thought of too — that I'd be the poor fool who was stuck in the shrubbery with nowhere to run when Dad came looking for revenge. If she'd been any kind of sister, she would have grabbed the hose again, but this wasn't Laura's style. She'd already scarpered to the safety of the kitchen. As I didn't fancy being soaked myself, there was only one thing I could do. Tiddles was still sitting on my back, purring and smelling like a manure heap on an off day. I reached back and took hold of him with one hand, throwing him as far out of the bushes as I could. This wasn't very far, because of how much the beast weighed, but it was far enough. I think it was something Dad had always dreamed of, coming face to face with his mortal enemy while he had a hose-pipe in his hand.

'So you're in it too, you feline Frankenstein,' he yelled in triumph.

I had time to see the jet of water catch Tiddles right up the tail before I was going backwards at the speed of light. Twigs, thorns, poisonous snakes, landmines, I didn't give a hoot for any of them. All I wanted to do was keep out of Dad's way and I didn't stop moving until I was in the kitchen. Mum and Laura were already there, holding each other up while they laughed fit to burst. Mum had the giggles so badly she was shaking all over.

'I suppose you all thought that was very funny.'

Dad had only been a few seconds behind me and it wasn't a very clever remark, considering the state the three of us were in. If I'd laughed any harder I'd have wet my pants, and Mum and Laura weren't any better. Dad really did look a sight with all his clothes sopping and a waterfall running off the end of his nose.

'It's all right,' Dad said, coming into the kitchen

and leaving great soggy footprints on the carpet tiles. 'I forgive you all.'

He proved it by giving Mum a great watery hug, which made her shriek. Laura and I both headed across the kitchen towards the door. Neither of us fooled ourselves that Dad would forget us, and he didn't.

'Don't rush off, my darling children,' Dad cooed, leering hideously at us while he still hugged poor Mum. 'I can see time must be hanging heavy on your hands. Laura, get some nail scissors, then go and cut the lawn. Tom, you can go and count how many pieces of gravel there are in the drive. Then you can polish them.'

''Fraid we can't, Dad,' Laura said over her shoulder, already halfway through the door. 'We have to meet someone. Bye.'

'Bye,' I echoed, following her out.

This was usually the way it went. Laura was the one in the lead while I tagged along behind.

Wroxford was as busy as it normally is on a Sunday afternoon. It is about half a mile from our house to the park and we didn't pass more than six people on the way. At the park entrance, Laura braked her bike to a halt and I pulled up behind her. Some boys from school were playing football just inside the railings and I gave them a wave. They waved back and went on with their game. None of them shouted for me to come along and join them. I wouldn't have gone anyway. Whenever I play football I either trip over my own feet or score in the wrong goal.

'Where are you going?' I asked.

I used 'you' deliberately. Laura and I get along

pretty well for a brother and sister but we don't live in each other's pockets. I have my friends and Laura has hers.

'We're going to make some money,' Laura told me.

'Cheerio then,' I said. 'I'll see you at teatime.'

Laura is always thinking of ways to make money, and none of them ever work. Three weeks back I'd spent a whole weekend collecting empty bottles with her. We had hundreds of the things, half-filling the garage, and Laura kept telling me we'd make pounds. We did make 36p at the local pub, but that was it. The only people who did well out of our efforts were those in charge of the local bottle bank. I'd promised myself then that I wouldn't have anything more to do with Laura's harebrained money-raising schemes. I would have ridden off but Laura pulled her bike out in front of mine and I had to stop. She grabbed my handlebars just to make sure I didn't escape.

'I know what you're thinking, Tom, but this time it's different. It really will work.'

'Sure,' I said. 'I hope you'll still speak to me when you're rich. Cheerio.'

I didn't do any better the second time than I had the first. Laura still had a death-grip on my handlebars and I didn't think Mum or Dad would appreciate it if I broke some of her fingers.

'You might at least listen to me.'

'OK, tell me.'

And then I'll clear off, I promised myself.

'Conkers,' she said.

'What does that mean, or are you trying to be rude?'

'Very funny, Tom. You know perfectly well what I

7

mean. We're going conkering and you're going to sell them at school tomorrow.'

This time I laughed out loud because there is only one horse chestnut tree in Wroxford. It grows in the park and there hadn't been a conker on it for weeks. In fact, most of them had gone before they were properly ripe. In Wroxford conkers are like gold dust.

'What are we going to do?' I asked. 'Camp out in the park until next autumn?'

'There's no need, Tom.' Laura was wearing the self-satisfied little smirk which never fails to irritate me. 'I know where there are thousands of conkers just waiting to be picked up.'

'I suppose the fairies at the bottom of the garden told you all about them.'

I mean, she must have thought I'd come down with the last shower of rain. Horse chestnut trees are about thirty metres tall. They're not exactly easy to hide.

'Let's just suppose I'm right. How much do you think the other boys would pay for them?'

'About 2p each.' The answer was there on the tip of my tongue. This was what Robby Attwell had charged when he'd brought a couple of pocketfuls back from holiday, and he'd sold the lot in five minutes. 'They'd have to be good ones, though.'

'These will be. Are you coming with me?'

'Where?'

'I don't want to spoil the surprise but it isn't far. We can be there in ten minutes.'

'You're not having me on?'

'Cross my heart and hope to die.'

So I went with her. There was only one thing that worried me. I believed Laura did know where there were some conkers, but for the life of me I couldn't understand why this should make her nervous. She'd tried to conceal it but I could tell. You can't hide much from a twin.

While Laura led me through the quiet streets, I tried to work out where she was taking me. I suppose the boys in Wroxford are pretty much like boys anywhere else. There are certain times of the year for doing things, football, cricket, tennis, swimming in the river and whatever. The one thing we didn't do a lot was play conkers, not because we didn't want to but because there simply weren't any around. The supply from the park lasted a few days and that was it. The little kids were so desperate to make sure they had their share, they knocked most of them out of the tree before they were ready. What puzzled me was that horse chestnut trees take years and years to grow. If there were some around, how come Laura was the only one to notice them? It didn't make sense, any more than that strange, frightened look in her eyes.

It was only when we turned up Runton Hill that I began to see the answer, and this was when I started to be frightened too. There were only two things at the top of the hill I knew about: miles and miles of open farmland that ran all the way to the coast — and the Manson house. Just thinking about it made me go all shivery inside.

The Manson house was haunted. It is a place where a lot of nasty things have happened. I was just like all the other kids who lived in Wroxford; I didn't want to go anywhere near the place. Of course, Mum and Dad and a lot of the other grown-ups laughed at the idea. They said all the stories about the house were superstition. That's grown-ups for you, though. If there was nothing wrong with the house, why hadn't anybody bought it? It had been standing empty for thirty years. Another thing, too. I'd noticed that if we ever went past the house at night, Dad always drove a little bit faster until it was safely behind us. Everybody did that.

It was a bad place to be, all right. It was a place where people had died in strange circumstances. Normally I'm not very good at history and I always have trouble remembering dates. Not with the Manson house, though. Thirty-first October 1958 was when it all started. This is a date which is as famous in Wroxford as 1066. Apparently the Manson family had lived in the town for years. Old Max, the caretaker at school, says it was the Mansons who turned Wroxford from a village into a town and for a long time they just about owned the place. They were the ones who built the big paper mill down by the river. Nearly all the shops in town used to have the name Manson over the door, and so had the bank. Wroxford had made the Mansons rich, and the house they built up on the hill overlooking town showed it. It was enormous and the gardens were bigger than our school playing field.

Then Gerald Manson happened along. All the Mansons before him had made money whatever they turned their hands to, but Gerald did the opposite. He kept on losing money until there was nothing left to lose. Eventually the worry must have sent him off his rocker because no normal person could have done what he did that Hallowe'en night. The servants had been given the night off and when they went in the next morning it must have been like 'A Nightmare on

Elm Street'. The Mansons' two children were dead in their beds and Mrs Manson was on the landing. They had been killed with a shotgun. Gerald Manson was in the library, where he'd shot himself with the same gun. Old Max did tell me once how he did it but it isn't something I like to think about. It's too horrible for words.

According to old Max, this was when people first began saying the spirit of Gerald Manson was still stalking the house. Some of them even said the house was cursed. They talked of flickering lights and shadows at the windows. One or two even claimed to have heard screaming at night, as though the ghost of Mrs Manson was still trying to escape from her husband.

Since then the house had stood empty, and nobody went near it unless they had to. The garden was completely overgrown, tiles were missing from the roof and the paint had all flaked off. You only had to look up at the house from the town to know there was something wrong with it. It was just standing there, waiting for new victims.

And it had had one. The stuff about the Mansons was something I'd heard. It was all ancient history. Little Jane Pomfret was somebody I knew about at first hand. It was almost two years ago the night she went missing and you may have heard about her yourself. It was on television and in all the newspapers. Four days the police were looking for her before the body was found and I'm not giving any prizes for guessing where it was. That's right, she was in the garden at the Manson house. All the reports say she died of cold and exhaustion but everybody in Wroxford knows better. I mean, how could a little kid

11

walk all that way without being seen by anybody? Out of all the gardens in Wroxford, why did it have to be the Manson house? No, we all knew Gerald Manson had claimed another victim. Just in case anybody doesn't believe me, there's one other thing I ought to say. It was Hallowe'en the night she went missing.

Perhaps you can understand now why I wasn't too keen on going anywhere near the Manson house with Laura. And that was where we were going, all right. The garden there was the only place some horse chestnut trees could possibly be hidden. As soon as I realized this, I put on a spurt and drew level with Laura.

'Let's stop a minute,' I said.

'What for? Are you out of puff?'

She was still nervous, I could tell, but she was excited as well. This is the funny thing about Laura. She can make herself do things, even when she's scared. Dad sometimes says she should have been a boy. It makes me wonder if he thinks I should have been a girl. I prefer to think I'm more sensible than Laura. She just says I've got a yellow streak.

'I want to talk,' I told her.

'Wait, until we're at the top of the hill. If we stop now, we'll have to push our bikes the rest of the way.'

She stood up on the pedals to give herself a bit of speed. The sensible thing would have been to let her go. If I had, if I'd turned back then, I'd have saved myself an awful lot of trouble. But 'ifs' don't count. I stood up on my pedals too and suddenly we were there, at the top of Runton Hill, with the rusty iron gates of the Manson house ahead of us. The house itself was hidden by the trees but I knew it was there. I was feeling shivery inside again.

'What did you want to talk about, Tom?'

Now it was too late, Laura had finally stopped.

'Those horse chestnut trees of yours,' I said. 'Are they in the Manson house garden?'

'That's right.'

'I can't see any.'

'They're on the far side of the garden. You can't see them from the road.'

'How do you know that?'

'I went in the garden last weekend.'

'On your own?'

Laura nodded and I was impressed. I also thought she was crazy. Wild horses wouldn't have dragged me in there on my own. They weren't going to drag me in with Laura either. I was scared enough where I was.

'What made you do it?' I asked.

'I wanted to see what it was like. Everybody is always talking about the Manson house and nobody I know has ever been there. I wanted to have a look.'

'Weren't you frightened?'

'I was petrified but I kept well clear of the house. Besides, it was broad daylight. I'm not sure I believe in ghosts, anyway, but if they do exist they only come out at night.'

I would have liked to see the written guarantee that said this. There were times when I was safe at home with Mum and Dad when I didn't believe in ghosts either. The trouble is, you're never really going to be sure unless you actually meet one. I preferred not to find out. I didn't want to go into the garden and bump into some evil spook who had got up early.

Laura was looking at me almost as though she was measuring me. I had a pretty good idea of what she could see because I guessed I looked the way I felt. If anyone had come up behind me and said 'Boo' I'd probably have had heart failure.

'There are thousands of conkers in there, Tom,' she said. 'They're just waiting for us to pick them up. Are you coming with me?'

'No.'

I was shaking my head hard just to make sure she had the message.

'You're too scared?'

'Yes.'

If she had taken the mickey out of me or called me a coward or something like that, this would have been the end of it. I'd have turned my bike round and cycled back to Wroxford. But Laura didn't. She simply nodded her head as though this was what she'd expected.

'All right,' she said quietly, 'I'll go and collect them on my own.'

She started cycling slowly towards the gates and for a few moments I simply watched her go. The thing was, I knew she was scared too. She didn't really want to go into that garden any more than I did, but she was forcing herself. It made me ashamed of myself.

'Wait a minute,' I called after her, my voice rather shaky. 'I've changed my mind.'

Although Laura was smiling back at me, I thought I was probably making a mistake. What I didn't know then was that I was doing the silliest thing I'd ever done in my life.

14

2

'Which way do we go?'

'Just follow me.'

For some reason we were both talking in whispers. The branches of the trees bordering the drive formed a kind of leafy ceiling and it was very dark. Perhaps it was my imagination, but it seemed unnaturally quiet as well. More than ever, I was convinced this wasn't a place I wanted to be. Even opening the gate into the garden had given me goose bumps. I'd always thought that only gates to cemeteries in horror movies creaked like that.

Laura was still forging ahead along the drive while I followed, keeping count of how many steps I'd have to run to get back to the road. I was so busy counting it took me a moment to realize we'd gone round a bend and the house was there in front of us. When I did, I stopped immediately. Even now, I can't put my finger on what was so frightening about it. I mean, I must have seen hundreds of big old buildings which weren't very different and I'd never given them a second thought. The Manson house was special, though. It looked so empty and unfriendly. It didn't want us there. I know this sounds daft. I know it was only a lot of bricks stuck together with a roof on top but it almost seemed to be alive. It was watching us and it didn't like what it could see. If the house had been able to speak, I knew just what it would have been saying. It would have been telling us to go away or it would be the worse for us.

'Hey, Laura,' I hissed. 'I thought we didn't have to go anywhere near the house.'

'We don't,' she told me. 'We go down here.'

She had kept walking and now she turned down a path to the left. Almost immediately she was out of sight, hidden by the bushes and trees, and I scurried after her. I don't think I could have stood being on my own. It was even darker on the path than it had been on the drive and I kept looking back over my shoulder, checking to make sure nothing was following us. I'm not sure exactly what I was afraid I'd see but I do know it would have been hideous.

Then I could see sunlight ahead of us and I started walking faster, almost treading on Laura's heels. I've never been more grateful to see a lawn before. It was huge, easily the size of a football pitch, and completely overgrown. More important, the sun was shining and there were no bushes for anything nasty to hide behind.

'There,' Laura said. 'I told you, didn't I?'

It was only now that I saw the horse chestnut trees. This shows the state I was in because they were pretty hard to miss. There were two of them growing in the middle of the overgrown lawn and they were enormous. They were also covered with nobbly green cases and I began to forget the terrors of a few seconds before. I knew there would be more of the cases beneath the trees and each case would contain a glossy conker. Even if I kept the best specimens for myself, I was looking at a small fortune.

'Come on,' Laura said. 'Let's get cracking.'

There were thousands of conkers on the ground, so

16

many there was no need to throw sticks up into the trees to knock more down. Laura had brought some plastic shopping bags with her and we set to work filling them, only taking the prime specimens. Busy as I was, I couldn't forget how close we were to the threat of the Manson house, and every few seconds I'd check to make sure there was nothing creeping up on us through the long grass. I also had something new to worry about. It was already late afternoon and the sun was sinking in the sky. Although it wouldn't be dark for a while, it would soon be dusk and we had the path and the drive to walk along.

Once we had the first two bags filled I'd have liked to leave, but a silly sort of pride stopped me saying anything. I was blowed if I'd show how nervous I was. I'd wait until Laura suggested we ought to go, even if this meant biting my tongue. So I went on cracking open the cases and putting the shiny conkers into the last of the bags. And I kept watching the sun sink lower in the sky.

At last the third bag was full. I looked across at Laura, half expecting her to produce another bag from somewhere, but she didn't.

'We'd better get going, Tom. It's starting to get dark.'

'Is it?' I said. 'I hadn't noticed.'

Although I'd tried to sound cool and casual, the little squeak in my voice let me down. Not that Laura noticed. She hadn't realized how dark it was getting and now she was nervous too. She didn't want to be around the Manson house after dark any more than I did.

We went back across the lawn far faster than we'd come but when we reached the path we had to slow down. This wasn't because of all the conkers we were carrying. It was because it was really dark under the trees. At first I couldn't see anything at all. Even when my eyes had adjusted, it wasn't much better. Laura was only a couple of paces ahead of me and I wouldn't have been able to see her at all if she hadn't been wearing a white top. Just to make matters worse, a breeze had got up. Leaves were rustling and branches were creaking all around us. At least, that's what I hoped it was. Otherwise there was a whole army of ghosts and ghouls surrounding us. One of them already had his icy fingers walking up and down my spine.

'Please hurry up, Laura,' I pleaded. 'Please don't take a wrong turn that leads us right up to the front door of the house, because old Gerald Manson will be waiting for us and. . . .'

This was as far as it went because I didn't want to think about what might happen next. In any case, all the pleading was inside my head. I was far too scared to speak out loud. Considering how dark it was on the path, Laura was doing a pretty good job. About the only way she could be sure she hadn't strayed off it was when she didn't crash into anything. Then she suddenly stopped. The first I knew of it was when my nose banged into the back of her neck.

'What's the matter?' I whispered shakily.

'Shush,' she answered.

I shushed. Laura was obviously listening for something so I listened too. All I could hear was the wind and the leaves and the branches and this great pounding sound which seemed to be getting closer and closer. I almost yelled out loud before I realized it was the pounding of my own heart that I could hear. By now I was even having difficulty breathing.

'I can't hear anything.'

'Nor can I now.' Laura sounded just as scared as I was. 'I thought I heard something moving in the bushes.'

'Great.' The squeak in my voice had grown until it was almost a shriek. 'Let's just stay where we are so whatever it is can catch us more easily.'

As I spoke, I gave Laura a shove in the back. This was all the urging she needed. Panic had set in and we were both running, regardless of the branches whipping at our faces and bodies like great skeletal claws. Twice I tripped on roots and nearly fell, but somehow I stayed on my feet and kept running. This time there was no looking back over my shoulder. I was too frightened of what I might see.

The only way we knew we'd reached the drive was by the crunch of gravel under our feet. It was almost as dark there as it had been on the path and for a moment we both paused to get our bearings. Although I didn't want to, something made me turn my head to the left, up towards the Manson house. In the semidarkness it was even more terrifying than it had been earlier, an ominous black bulk silhouetted against the early evening sky. I could almost feel the evil reaching out towards me. And then, while I was watching, it happened. Without warning a flickering light appeared at one of the downstairs windows, and behind it I could see a crooked, shadowy shape. Someone, or something, was looking out at us, and the blood seemed to freeze in my veins. This time it was Laura's turn to give me a shove.

'Run, Tom,' she screamed. 'Run for your life.'

There was no need for her to tell me a second time.

It was daylight again outside the gates. At least, it was evening light but we'd left the darkness of the path and drive behind us. I hoped we'd left other things behind us as well. Although I kept running hard until I reached the bikes, once I was there I stopped to wait for Laura. After I'd checked that nothing horrible had followed us out of the garden, that is. By now I had my panic more or less under control, even if my heart was still pumping away like a steam hammer.

'We're all right now,' Laura panted.

'Sure,' I agreed. 'Let's get pedalling.'

My panic wasn't that far below the surface. I wanted to put distance between myself and the Manson house.

'There's no rush. Let me get my breath back first.'

This was when she screamed. Not Laura, the woman in the house — if it was a woman. It's very difficult to tell whether screams are male or female. All I knew, or wanted to know, was that someone or something in the Manson house was in mortal terror. It was infectious, and all the hairs on the back of my neck were standing up on end. There was no need for discussion with Laura. We swapped one frightened glance, then we were both on our bikes, pumping the pedals for all we were worth.

When it came to running away, Laura was the one who had to follow me. I went down the hill faster than I've ever travelled on a bike before. Every bend was an adventure, with me wobbling crazily all over the road, but I didn't slow down until we reached the first houses of Wroxford. It was nice to know there were other people nearby, real live people. At the main road I stopped, letting Laura pull alongside. Considering the speed I'd been going, she hadn't been doing at all badly. She couldn't have been more than twenty metres behind.

'I didn't know you could go that fast, Tom.'

'Nor did I,' I admitted. 'It's amazing what you can do when you have to.'

For a minute or two we just sat there and panted companionably, getting our nerves back under control.

'Do you know something?' Laura said once her breathing was normal again. 'We behaved like a couple of babies.'

'What do you mean?' I was quite indignant.

'Well, what exactly were we running away from?'

'A ghost,' I told her. 'A great slavering ghoul that would have torn us limb from limb.'

'Don't be so silly, Tom. I didn't see a ghost.'

'Yes you did. It was there in the window.'

'We saw somebody with a lamp,' Laura corrected me. 'It might have been a tramp looking for somewhere warm to spend the night.'

'And if we both look up, we might see a pig flying over. What about the scream?'

'That could have been a bird or the wind or something.'

The trouble was, Laura was right. The scream had been a long way away and, the state I'd been in, almost anything would have started me running again. And what exactly had I seen at the window? There had been a flickering light all right, and there had definitely been a shadow, but I hadn't hung around to do any checking. I mean, I was hardly

21

going to walk up to the window and say 'Excuse me but are you a ghost?' So it could have been some old tramp. Then I shivered. Deep down inside I knew just what I'd seen and heard, and it certainly hadn't been anything natural.

There wasn't any chance to argue the toss with Laura. It was really beginning to get dark now, but even in the dim light it was impossible to mistake the expression on her face. When she's really angry, her face goes all blotchy, and this was the way she looked now.

'Tom Venables,' she said, and her voice wasn't exactly full of admiration, 'where are your conkers?'

Although I did think of making a joke of it, I quickly changed my mind. I felt too ashamed. Laura's bag was still there, hanging on the handle-bars. She'd kept it, even when we were racing down the hill. My two bags were gone.

'I don't know,' I said miserably. 'They seem to have gone missing.'

'That's typical.' Laura wasn't about to let it go. 'I slave away all afternoon and you mess it up.'

'I'm sorry.'

'Sorry isn't good enough.'

This was something she'd borrowed from Mum, and now I was starting to get angry myself. OK, I may have lost the conkers but I'd had a reason. It wasn't every day I was chased by ghosts.

'I tell you what,' I said. 'I'm pretty sure I dropped the bags on the drive. Why don't you pop back to the Manson house and collect them. As you said, there's nothing to worry about up there.'

Laura just sniffed and stuck her nose up in the air before she started cycling towards home. I followed more slowly. One thing was for sure, though. I wasn't going back to get the conkers. They could stay there until they rotted, because I was never going near the Manson house again. Never, never, never.

This all goes to show how wrong you can be.

The next morning Laura wasn't the only person who was angry with me for dropping the bags. I was angry with myself as well. I'd known all along that plenty of the boys would want the conkers but I hadn't realized how many they would want to buy. And it wasn't just the boys, either. A lot of the girls were in the market for them as well. I don't think the school tuck shop did any business during morning play because all the kids were spending everything they had with me. Oliver Battersby was my best customer — he bought 50p worth — but there were lots of others who spent 10p and 20p. It made me wish I'd charged a bit more.

I did the selling round the back of one of the mobiles, out of sight of the teacher on duty, while Laura kept watch. Not that I thought I was doing anything wrong. I mean, I wasn't ripping anybody off or anything. The trouble is, you can never be sure with grown-ups, and that goes double for teachers. It was best to be on the safe side.

Most of the conkers went during the morning break and I shifted the rest at lunchtime. Apart from a few I kept in the bag for people who had promised to bring the money the next day, they had all gone. Both Laura and me were feeling pretty pleased with ourselves. If she was remembering the bags I'd lost, she wasn't saying anything more about it. She was far more interested in the money.

'How much have we made, Tom?'

'I don't know. I didn't have time to keep count.'

'Make a guess then.'

'Well, we've made at least five pounds.'

I thought we'd probably made at least twice as much. All my pockets were so full of coins I could hardly walk.

'They must be crazy.'

This wasn't Laura, it was Ali Baba. Alistair Barber was his real name, but nobody called him Alistair except his harem. Ali was a born-again nerd. He'd only moved to Wroxford a few weeks before and already there wasn't a boy in the school who could stand him. He was one of those smart-aleck know-alls who manage to put everybody's back up. Mind you, the teachers loved him and so did a lot of the girls. Laura had been making gooey eyes at him with the best of them when Ali first turned up, but this hadn't lasted very long. Although I'd have liked to think she had more sense than the others, it had more to do with Bianca Allen than anything else. Laura and Bianca were sworn enemies. Ever since Laura had seen Ali walking home from school with Bianca, she hadn't had a civil word to say about him.

Anyway, I'd noticed Ali hanging around while I was selling the conkers, looking superior the way he usually did. I'd been hoping he'd ask to buy a few himself. Then I could have told him I was only selling to friends. But he hadn't. He'd simply hung around until I closed up shop, so he could invite himself into our conversation. This all went to show what a sensitive person he was. He must have known Laura and me found him about as appealing as a fresh cowpat.

'Who's crazy?' I asked.

Although I didn't like him, I was still polite because that's the way I am. Besides, Ali was quite a bit bigger than me and he'd told everybody he was a black belt in karate. Nobody believed him, of course, but there was always an outside chance he was telling the truth. I'm about as good at fighting as I am at football.

'All those people who were buying conkers,' Ali explained. 'It's stupid.'

'Why?'

Unlike me, Laura was quite happy for Ali to know she couldn't abide him.

'You don't have to pay for conkers. You pick them up from under horse chestnut trees.'

'Not around here, you don't,' I said. 'There aren't any trees.'

'So where did you get yours from? I suppose you had them specially imported.'

It was the stupid little laugh which really got up my nose. I can't stand people who laugh at their own jokes, especially when they're not very funny.

'No,' I told him. 'We got them from the garden of the Manson house.'

'Is that the place on the hill that's supposed to be haunted?'

'That's the one, and that's the reason people were buying the conkers. No one, apart from Laura and me, has got the guts to go up there.'

This wasn't quite true. After all, nobody except Laura and me knew there were any horse chestnut trees in the garden and I couldn't pretend that dropping the bags of conkers when I ran away was very heroic. The trouble was, Ali was making me annoyed.

'In that case,' he said in that toffee-nosed voice of his, 'they're even more stupid than I thought. There are no such things as ghosts.'

Ali turned away and started to walk into the playground. Although I wasn't sorry to see him go, Laura must have thought differently. She hadn't said anything for a while, which was unnatural for her. Now she decided to make up for it.

'So you're not frightened of ghosts?' she said.

'Of course I'm not.' Ali had stopped again. 'You can't be frightened of something which doesn't exist.'

'You mean you'd go up to the Manson house?'

'Why not? It's only a building.'

'After dark?'

'What difference would that make? It's only little babies who are afraid of the dark.'

'How about going there on Wednesday, on Hallowe'en night?'

'That wouldn't make any difference either. Hallowe'en is simply another superstition.'

'OK, Alistair,' Laura said, her eyes sparkling. 'That's what I dare you to do, to go up to the Manson house on Wednesday night.'

'I don't accept dares,' Ali told her. 'My dad says they're childish.'

'I knew it,' I said. 'He really is all mouth.'

This wasn't at all polite. From the way Ali was glaring at me, I thought I was about to discover whether the karate story was true or not.

'I'm not scared,' he said. 'I just don't want to do it, that's all.'

'All right, Alistair,' Laura said sweetly, putting the knife in. 'I believe you. You've told us lots of times how brave and clever and strong you are, so it must

26

be true. The thing is, will all the other boys and girls understand when I tell them about the dare?'

For a second or two I almost felt sorry for Ali. He'd opened his big mouth once too often and he'd talked himself into a position where he couldn't possibly win. Either he accepted the dare or everybody would know he was nothing but hot air. He'd be labelled chicken for the rest of his time at the school.

'I'm really not scared of ghosts,' he said, almost pleading.

'Prove it then,' Laura told him, her voice like syrup.

For a long moment Ali just stood there. Then he slowly nodded his head.

'I'll do it,' he said. 'I'll go to the Manson house on Hallowe'en night, but I still think it's childish.'

This time we didn't try to call him back when he walked away. Instead, Laura and me just stood there and looked at each other. I think we were both wondering what we'd done.

3

'That's a great mask,' Dad said. 'Really frightening. My heart stopped beating for a second when I first saw it.'

'I'm not wearing a mask,' I said patiently.

Although Dad has a great sense of humour most of the time, there are occasions when he goes a bit over the top.

'Aren't you, Tom?' Dad leaned forward to peer more closely. 'Oh no, I can see you aren't now. There is something different about you, though.'

'Tom has just had a bath,' Mum chipped in.

'Good Lord, that must account for it then. I hadn't realized the anniversary had come round again. Mind you, I still don't understand it. How can a good-looking fellow like me have spawned an ugly son like you?'

'It's funny you should mention that,' I said. 'Everybody says I'm the spitting image of you but with a bit more hair.'

There was a little snort of laughter from Mum, and Dad pretended to cuff me round the ear. His bald patch had started to spread across the top of his head and he didn't like it.

Just then Laura wandered in. I'd been waiting for her for at least ten minutes, wondering how anybody could possibly take so long to put on a pair of jeans and a woolly. She'd probably been checking her face for spots again.

'Where are you two off to?' Dad asked. 'Are you trick and treating?'

'Something like that,' Laura told him.

She'd chosen her words carefully. Although we'd both been brought up not to lie, we were both very good at not telling the entire truth.

'Well, don't be late back,' Mum said. 'Hallowe'en or not, you still have to go to school tomorrow.'

'We won't be,' I promised, herding Laura towards the door. 'Bye.'

Not that I was really in that much of a hurry to go. Ever since Monday I'd been hoping Laura would forget about the silly dare. In fact, I'd been very careful not to mention it at all, but I'd been wasting my time. This morning she'd collared Ali and reminded him that the three of us had a date. My last hope had died when Ali failed to come up with an excuse. If it had been me, Mum would have been on her deathbed or the parrot having kittens. I'd have found some way to wriggle out of it, but not Ali. He simply asked where we were supposed to meet and when. Perhaps the silly pillock really wasn't scared of ghosts. I was, though. I didn't want to go anywhere near the Manson house again, especially not after dark on Hallowe'en night.

'Look, Laura,' I said, once we were out in the garage collecting our bikes. 'Do you think we ought to go through with this?'

'Why shouldn't we?'

'Well, it does seem a bit mean.'

'There's nothing mean about it. Nobody forced Mr Cleverclogs Barber to open his big mouth. He's brought it on himself.'

Although this wasn't strictly true, I recognized the

29

mood Laura was in and I didn't bother to argue. I tried changing tack instead.

'OK,' I said. 'Let Ali go up there if he wants to. That's no reason for us to go as well.'

'Oh yes there is, Tom Venables. I'm going to be there to make sure he really does it. I want to see just how brave he is.'

Laura had her bike unlocked and she started to push it out of the garage. I followed after her, feet as heavy as lead. My very last hope was that Ali Baba wouldn't be where we had arranged to meet him.

Ali was not only there, he had his classy new bike with him, drop handlebars and all. He also had what looked like a new watch. I had a chance to notice it because he was sitting directly beneath a streetlamp and he checked his watch carefully when we arrived.

'You're late,' he said.

'We were giving you a chance to think,' I said. 'It's not too late to back out, you know.'

I thought this sounded better than saying anything about Laura and her zit hunt. It also meant I didn't get kicked.

'Why would I want to back out?' Ali sounded as though he really meant it. 'All I want to do is get this over with. I've got a lot of homework to finish.'

'You might not be able to finish it,' I warned him. 'After tonight you might not be doing any more homework at all.'

'Don't be so silly. Are you two going in front? I'm not sure of the way.'

We went in front, leading him out of Wroxford and up Runton Hill. Ali was whistling happily behind us, as though he didn't have a care in the world. As for me, I was becoming more nervous with every turn of the pedals. OK, there was a bright moon and I wouldn't have to go into the garden, but I'd still be far too close to the Manson house for comfort. Too many nasty things had happened there at Hallowe'en for this to be a coincidence. Besides, what Laura and me had seen the previous Sunday was fresh in my memory. It made me feel bad about what we were doing to Ali. He might not have a care in the world, but I was worrying enough for both of us. When we reached the top of the hill, I dropped back to ride beside him.

'Look,' I said, speaking in a low voice so Laura wouldn't overhear. 'You really don't have to go through with this. Nobody will call you chicken.'

'You don't think I've ridden all this way for nothing, do you?' He just didn't want to be helped. 'Besides, I might decide to be childish myself. I might have a dare for you and your precious sister later on.'

I had a pretty good idea of what the dare would be and, despite myself, I shivered. One thing was definite. The whole world could go 'cluck-cluck-cluck' whenever they saw me, but I wasn't going anywhere nearer to the Manson house than the road. Mind you, I did go a bit closer than I'd intended. Laura and me would have stopped where we had on Sunday but Ali kept riding until we were bang opposite the gates.

'So this is it,' Ali said.

'That's right.'

My voice was letting me down again, the way it always did when I was frightened. It was going all squeaky and Ali wasn't slow to notice.

'What's the matter, Tom?' In the moonlight I

could see Ali was grinning. 'You're not scared, are you?'

'Of course I'm not,' I squeaked.

'If you remember, Tom has already been in the garden,' Laura pointed out.

No matter how much Laura and me squabbled in private, we always stood up for each other when outsiders were around.

'That was in daylight. This time it's after dark. And it's Hallowe'en, the night when all the ghosts and spirits come out to play.'

'I thought you didn't believe in ghosts,' Laura said.

'I don't. I was just trying to cheer Tom up. What exactly do you want me to do?'

There were two reasons I kept quiet. One was that I didn't want to go all squeaky again. The other was that I wasn't really sure what Laura had in mind.

'You go up the drive, Alistair,' she told him, 'and knock at the front door.'

'Is anybody going to answer it?' Ali was grinning again.

'For your sake, I hope not,' Laura said solemnly.

'And that's all I have to do, knock at the door? It hardly seems worth the effort of cycling up here.'

'There's one other thing. If nobody does answer the door, you're to shout out "Gerald Manson, I've come to visit you".'

'That's stupid.'

'It's part of the dare,' Laura told him.

'That doesn't make it any less stupid. I'll do it, though, just to keep you two idiots happy. See you in a minute.'

Ali started off across the road towards the gate, pushing his bike with him.

'You can leave your bike with us,' I said. 'We'll look after it.'

'No thanks. I'm going to need it.'

'What, so you can run away faster?'

For one glorious moment I really thought Ali was beginning to crack.

'Don't be so daft.' Perhaps I was wrong but I had the feeling Ali didn't have a very high opinion of me. 'It's pitch-dark under those trees. I'm going to need the light to find my way up the drive.'

I half expected Laura to say it was part of the dare to go up to the house in absolute darkness, but she didn't. She just stood beside me and watched Ali open the gate. It squeaked as hideously for him as it had for us on Sunday. This made me wonder who had closed it again. Laura and me certainly hadn't stopped to do it when we left.

Once Ali was inside, he turned and gave us a little wave before he got on his bike and started cycling up the drive. The cocky so-and-so was actually whistling as he went. For a while we could see the beam of his front light cutting a narrow yellow tunnel through the darkness. Then he turned a bend and was gone from sight. It was as though he had never been with us. I knew this was silly but it made me uncomfortable.

'How long do you think he'll be?' I asked.

'I don't know,' Laura answered. 'It all depends what happens to him up at the house.'

'Do you think something will?' My voice was squeaking again.

'I hope not.'

Laura's voice didn't sound quite right either. Even in the moonlight, I could see she was just as scared as I was. She didn't mind showing it, either. When she held out her hand, it was for me to comfort her, but this worked both ways. When I grabbed hold of it, I was looking out for my own selfish interests. It was pathetic really, the two of us standing there in the moonlight, holding hands like a couple of little kids. An owl hooted nearby and I could feel Laura jump. She would have been able to feel me do the same because I went about a metre higher. Although both of us wanted nothing more than to turn tail and run home the way we had on Sunday, we couldn't. We'd sent Ali up to the Manson house and now we had to wait for him to come back.

If he was going to come back, because he seemed to have been gone for an awfully long time. I kept hoping to see the light from his bicycle light on the bushes, but I didn't. The garden remained as dark and silent as a. . . . Suddenly I was shivering again, all over from head to toe. The word I'd been thinking of was 'grave', and it was dead bodies which went in graves before they became ghosts. The thought didn't do anything to calm my nerves.

'Shouldn't Ali be back by now?' I asked.

'That was what I was thinking.'

For a moment neither of us spoke. Then I phrased the question which was uppermost in both our minds.

'Laura,' I said, my voice almost a whisper. 'Do you think something has stopped him coming back?'

'No.' Although Laura was shaking her head, she didn't sound very convincing. 'He's probably just messing around. Give him a shout.'

I didn't want to. I knew it was silly, but if there *was* something in the house, I didn't want to attract its attention. I'd rather it didn't know I was there.

'You do it, Laura,' I said. 'It's your idea.'

'Let's both shout together.'

So we shouted, not very loudly at first but doing better with each attempt. After five or six goes we gave up. Although Ali should have been able to hear us, there had been no answer. I tried not to think of the possible reasons for this. All the same, I kept a careful eye on the gates. If anything apart from Ali came down the drive, I'd be off down the hill at two hundred miles an hour.

'He's probably waiting just round the corner in the drive,' Laura said. 'And laughing his head off.'

'That would be just like him,' I agreed.

I didn't believe this for a minute and I don't think Laura did either. Another few minutes dragged by and there was still no sign of Ali. We tried shouting again, but all we heard in reply was the sighing of the breeze in the trees. By now I was pretty sure in my mind that Ali wouldn't be coming back.

'What are we going to do?' I was on the verge of panic. If anything had happened to Ali, it was our fault.

'I don't know. Do you think we ought to go up to the house to look for him?'

'No, I don't.' I made this very definite.

'I think we have to, Tom. We can't just leave him.'

'You're not thinking straight.' It was amazing how quickly my brain worked when I was scared out of my wits. The reasons for keeping away from the Manson house had popped into my mind without any effort. 'If Ali is still up at the house, he must have

35

heard us shouting. Either he doesn't want to answer us or he can't. If he can't, that means something nasty must have happened to him. It doesn't make sense for us to have the same nasty thing happen to us. We ought to go and fetch help.'

Laura had started laughing before I finished. I knew I hadn't expressed myself very well but I couldn't remember saying anything amusing. For a moment I was sure she must be hysterical and I wondered whether I ought to slap her face. The trouble was, I knew she'd slap me back — and Laura packs a pretty mean punch for a girl.

'What's the matter?' I asked.

'I've just realized what fools we are.' There was laughter and relief in Laura's voice. 'While we're standing here like a pair of prize idiots, Alistair is probably back home.'

'What do you mean?'

Laura wasn't simply hysterical, she'd lost her marbles as well. There was no way Ali could have come out of the garden without us seeing him.

'It's obvious, when you think about it. That's why Alistair wouldn't leave his bike with us. He just cycled down the drive, past the house and out of the other gate.'

'What other gate?'

'The one on the far side of the garden. It leads on to the back road.'

Laura was right. I hadn't been along the back road very often, mainly because it didn't really go any-where. Now she mentioned it, though, I could vaguely remember a small gate in the wall.

'So you think that's what he's done?'

'I'm sure of it. Come on, Tom. Let's get going.

We've wasted enough time hanging around here.'

When Laura left, I went with her. Let's face it, almost any excuse would have been good enough to persuade me away from the Manson house, but I wasn't convinced. Although what Laura said sounded reasonable, I couldn't rid myself of the uncomfortable feeling that this wasn't the real explanation. I mean, how could Ali know about the other gate? He'd only been in Wroxford a few weeks and he hadn't even been sure of the way up Runton Hill.

The more I thought about this, the more uncomfortable I became. The dare might have been Laura's idea but I'd gone along with it. I wanted to be sure Ali was all right. Even if I didn't like him very much, I certainly didn't wish him any harm. The first telephone box I saw once we were back in town made me call out to Laura to stop.

'What are you doing?' she asked.

'I'm going to phone up Ali and make sure he's all right.'

'How are you going to do that?'

'It's quite easy really.' Sometimes I could be as sarcastic as Dad. 'This thing beside us is called a phone box. Look inside and you'll see this gadget made of black plastic. If you —'

'I know all that,' Laura said impatiently. 'What I want to know is how you're going to find the number.'

'Haven't you ever heard of a telephone directory?'

'Of course I have, but Alistair has only just moved to Wroxford. His number won't be in there yet. In any case, there are about five million Barbers in the directory. Do you know where Alistair lives?'

'Not really.'

To be honest, I didn't have a clue.

'In that case, Directory Enquiries won't be any help either. Besides, even if you did manage to get through, you'd only give Alistair another good laugh. He'll have been home for hours by now.'

Laura didn't seem to have any doubts at all. I could only hope she was right.

4

Ali wasn't at school the next day. Although I hung around in the playground after the bell had gone, waiting until the last stragglers had drifted in through the gates, there wasn't a sign of him. Just to make absolutely sure, I asked to go to the loo while Mr Langley was taking the register. I only had to wait in the toilets for a minute or so before Carl Masters came wandering in to check the grease on his hair hadn't turned rancid. With the gel making his hair stick up every which way, he looked like a mobile lavatory brush. He thought this made him look cool. I thought it made him look a right prat, but this was an opinion I kept to myself. Carl had orang-utan blood in his veins. He had these great muscled arms that hung most of the way to his knees and he was about twice my size. This made him the kind of person I was always very polite to.

'Hello, Tom.' Carl might be big and ugly but he was pretty amiable, provided you kept on the right side of him. 'What are you doing? Are you skipping assembly as well?'

'No,' I told him. 'I just fancied a wander. Have you seen Ali around?'

Carl and Ali were in the same class.

'Don't tell me you two have become buddy-buddy.'

'You must be joking.' Carl wasn't an Ali fan either. 'He said something about buying conkers.'

39

'I didn't know you had any left.'

'There's only a few.'

'Well you can cross Ali off your list of customers. He isn't at school today.'

This was all I wanted from Carl. I chatted for a few seconds, just to be sociable, and then I went back to class. I didn't have a chance to talk to Laura until after assembly. She was with a group of her friends but I managed to cut her out from the herd.

'Ali isn't at school,' I told her.

'So?' Laura didn't sound particularly concerned.

'For goodness sake,' I said. 'You know where he went last night. Ali went up to the Manson house with us and he didn't come back.'

'There's only one reason he didn't come back with us. He kept right on going out of the other gate.'

'But he isn't at school, Laura.' I was almost pleading with her. 'How do you account for that?'

'Easily. He's probably caught that stomach bug that's going around. Either that or he's stayed away deliberately to wind us up.'

Although there was quite a lot more I'd have liked to say, I wasn't given the chance. Laura had already turned on her heel and was off to rejoin her friends. This is one of the few things I don't like about her. I mean, she is really great to have as a sister, not a bit soppy like some of the other girls, and she is jolly good company most of the time. Unfortunately, she has this one blind spot. When something nasty or unpleasant comes along, she turns her back on it. She ducks and squirms and does just about anything to avoid facing up to it.

This was what she was doing now. And she was still ducking and squirming at playtime. Although I

40

had a good look around, I couldn't find her anywhere. I guessed she was hiding in the girls' toilets to
avoid me.

For want of anything better to do, I wandered
down to see old Max. The caretaker's room is
supposed to be out of bounds, but there are one or
two of us that Max doesn't mind coming for a visit.
Getting there is dead easy. All you have to do is wait
until the teacher on duty turns his back, run down a
short flight of stairs, duck round a corner and you are
home and dry.

I found old Max doing what he usually seems to be
doing: sitting at the table in his room, a cup of tea on
the table in front of him and one of his vile hand-
rolled cigarettes hanging out of his mouth. When he
saw me, he waved me to the other chair at the table. I
sat down and waited while the cigarette burned down
almost all the way to his lips. There are some days
when you can't get Max to stop talking and others
when he won't say a word. The way to get on with
him is to play by his rules. If he wants to talk, you
talk. If he doesn't, you sit in silence.

'You're looking like a wet weekend, Thomas,' he
said at last.

He was the only person who ever called me
Thomas. Although I hated it, I'd never said so to
him.

'I'm sorry.'

'There's no need to apologize for being miserable,
boy. What's bothering you?'

'It's the Manson house.'

'Ah.'

Old Max nodded his head and went back to saying
nothing. I sat and watched the cigarette burn down,

waiting for the yell of pain as it blistered his lips. It didn't happen, of course, it never does. My theory is that the end he holds in his lips is so wet and soggy, the cigarette goes out of its own accord.

'There aren't many places that are really evil,' he said suddenly, removing the cigarette from his mouth and dropping it in the old tin he used as an ashtray, 'but the Manson house is one of them. It's a place to steer well clear of all right.'

'Do you really believe all the stories?'

Old Max laughed, his adam's apple bobbing up and down his scrawny neck.

'Believe them?' he said. 'Any stories you've heard are only the tip of the iceberg. And there's worse to come, believe you me. This is one of the bad times.'

'What do you mean?'

'Lights have been seen at the windows at night,' Max explained. 'People going by have heard un- earthly screams. That always spells trouble for somebody.'

Although it was quite warm, my teeth were beginning to chatter like a set of castanets. I mean, I was one of those who had seen the light and heard the screams.

'Max,' I began.

I intended to tell him everything, but as I spoke the bell rang for the end of play.

'I'd better be off,' I finished.

Although Mr Langley isn't a bad sort, the one sure way to upset him is to be late for one of his classes.

I saw the police car when I came up the steps from old Max's cubbyhole. It was parked outside the main entrance to the school, a uniformed policeman at the wheel. I didn't think too much of it at the time because I was making sure Miss Everett didn't see me. She was the teacher on duty and we'd already had one or two little run-ins about me being in places I shouldn't. She had a way of talking to you when she was angry which made you feel knee-high to a sparrow.

Anyway, it wasn't until about twenty minutes later that the world caved in. Langley was droning on as usual and most of us in the class were trying not to yawn too obviously when the door opened and Mr Hewitt walked in. He is the headmaster and we don't usually see much of him except at assemblies. If he comes into one of the classrooms, this normally means trouble for somebody, so nobody felt like cheering when he appeared. We just jumped to our feet and wondered who the unlucky one was.

'I'm sorry to disturb you, Mr Langley,' Hewitt said, 'but I have somebody with me who would like a brief word with the class. Will that be all right?'

'Of course it will, Mr Hewitt.'

Mr Langley didn't actually lick the headmaster's shoes but he came pretty close. Although he'd asked permission politely enough, Mr Hewitt had expected only one answer.

'Thank you, Mr Langley. Perhaps you'd like to come in, Inspector Venables.'

There was this horrible sinking sensation in my stomach. There weren't many times when I wasn't pleased to see Dad, but this was definitely one of them because I knew why he was there. Even so, I couldn't help noticing how different he seems once he is dressed for work. When he is slobbing around at home in a pair of jeans and a sweatshirt, he isn't much different from anybody else's dad. Put him in his uniform, though, and this all changes. Then you notice how big and strong and dependable he is. I don't think I could ever be afraid of anything if he was there with me. Unless he was angry with me, of course, and this was precisely what he was likely to be in a very few moments.

'Thank you very much, Mr Hewitt,' Dad said, using his official voice. 'Now children, I want you to listen carefully because I need your help. I believe all of you know Alistair Barber.'

Everyone in the class nodded their heads. At least, nearly everybody did. All the muscles in my body seemed to be frozen, not just the ones in my neck, and I simply sat and stared across at where Laura was sitting. Her head wasn't nodding either. She was sitting very still and her face had gone deathly pale. I didn't need to be her twin to know what she was thinking. Like me, she'd be offering up a prayer that Ali was all right. I didn't think I could bear it if Dad mentioned anything about finding Ali's body.

'The thing is,' Dad went on, 'nobody seems to know where Alistair is. His parents haven't seen him since early yesterday evening and he didn't go home at all last night. As you can imagine, Mr and Mrs Barber are almost out of their minds with worry.'

They weren't the only ones. Every word seemed to be another nail hammered into me. Whatever had happened to Ali was all my fault. I'd never felt quite so guilty and miserable in my life.

'As far as we know, Alistair left his home at about half-past seven last night.' After a brief pause to let the significance of what he'd said sink in, Dad was off again. 'He was on his bike. After that, what happened to him is a complete mystery. We have no idea where he went or what he did. I'm hoping some of you may be able to help us fill in the gap. Did any of you see Alistair Barber after half-past seven last night? Better still, do any of you know where he might have gone?'

I was still frozen in my seat but a girl's hand had already shot up. It wasn't Laura's.

'What's your name?' Dad asked.

'Karen, sir. Karen Smith.'

'And what do you know, Karen?'

'I don't really know anything, sir. It's just that I saw Alistair last night. He was cycling along Gardenia Avenue.'

'What time was this, Karen?'

'About a quarter to eight, sir.'

Karen always started blushing when she had to answer a question in class. By now her face was brick red.

'Did you say anything to him?'

'No, sir. He was on the far side of the road.'

'I see. Did you happen to notice which way he turned at the end of the avenue?'

'I think he went left, sir, but I can't really be sure. I wasn't really paying that much attention. I'm sorry, sir.'

'That's all right, Karen. You've been a great help. Is there anybody else who can add anything to what she's told me?'

Nobody else moved and there was no avoiding the moment of truth any longer. Slowly, ever so slowly, I raised my hand. Out of the corner of my eye I could see that Laura's hand had gone up too. For a second Dad didn't speak.

'All right, Tom,' he said at last. 'What can you tell me?'

'I know where Ali — I mean Alistair — was last night.' My voice was squeaking away like mad. 'He was with Laura and me. We went up to the Manson house.'

Even with Mr Hewitt there, nothing could stop the little buzz of excitement which went round the classroom. Although I knew everybody's eyes were on me, it was only Dad who mattered. He simply nodded his head before he turned to the headmaster.

'Is it all right if I take Tom and Laura out of class for a few minutes?' he asked. 'I think this is best discussed in private.'

'Of course, Inspector. I'm sure Mr Langley won't mind.'

He didn't, and in a matter of seconds the four of us were outside in the corridor. Mr Hewitt loaned Dad his office, then we were down to three.

'For goodness sake, you two,' Dad said once we were alone. 'It's me, your father. You're not facing a firing squad. You haven't done anything wrong, have you?'

'I don't know,' I said miserably.

'If we have, we didn't mean to,' Laura added.

'That sounds ominous. You'd better tell me all about it.'

One thing about Dad, he is a great listener. It is probably part of his job but he is always easy to talk to. With a little prompting from him, we told him everything about the previous night, right down to the smallest detail. Once we'd finished, Dad didn't say anything for a few moments. I didn't mind. I just felt relieved to have it off my chest.

'OK,' Dad said. 'You made this silly dare and the three of you cycled up to the Manson house. Alistair went inside while you two waited outside the gate. When he didn't come back, you rode off home.'

'That's right,' I agreed.

'You simply left him there?'

'We tried shouting for him,' Laura pointed out.

'Why didn't you go in to look for him when he didn't answer?'

'We thought he must have slipped out another way,' Laura said.

'We were scared,' I said at the same moment.

Although Dad only nodded, I think it was my explanation he believed.

'All right, let me ask you something. Now you know Alistair has disappeared, what do you think has happened to him?'

Laura and me just looked at each other, neither of us wanting to admit what we thought.

'Come on, you two,' Dad prompted. 'You must have some thoughts about it.'

'I think something nasty happened to him at the Manson house,' I said, once I realized Laura wasn't going to bail me out.

'What kind of nasty?' Dad asked. 'Are you talking about ghosts?'

It sounded awfully silly, sitting there in the headmaster's office with the sunshine streaming in the window. All the same, I'd rather sound silly than lie to Dad.

'It was the ghosts,' I told him.

'Is that what you think too?'

'Yes,' Laura answered. Her voice was almost a whisper.

'In that case, we'd better go up to the Manson house and see whether these ghosts of yours left any clues behind. Come along, you two.'

It seemed we were going to be out of Mr Langley's class for more than a few minutes.

'Tell me what happened,' Dad said.

He was sitting in the front seat, twisted round so he could speak to Laura and me. PC Wren, the driver, had parked almost exactly where we'd been standing the previous night.

'This is where we stayed,' I said.

'All the time?'

'Yes.'

'Even when you were shouting to Alistair, you didn't go any closer?'

'No. We stayed here.'

It seemed strange for me to be doing all the talking while Laura was around. She'd been unnaturally quiet ever since we left school. I guessed she must be sickening for something.

'What did Alistair do?'

'He went straight across the road and in at the gate.'

'Taking his bicycle with him. Did he say why?'

'It was dark in the drive under the trees. He said he needed the light.'

'That makes sense.' Dad was nodding his head. 'It's pretty gloomy even now. Come on. Let's trace his footsteps.'

The gate to the Manson house squeaked just as much now as it had done previously, but this didn't seem nearly so menacing with Dad and another large policeman beside us. I wasn't even nervous as I walked up the drive. Mind you, my first sight of the house itself was worth a goose bump or two. What old Max had told me leapt back into my mind. He'd said it was an evil place, and I still agreed with him. The house was as scary and unwelcoming as ever, but today I didn't feel it posed any threat to me. Perhaps it was because Dad was with me. Or perhaps it was because the house already had a victim. This was a thought which brought out a few more goose bumps.

Even so, I didn't break stride. Dad was going all the way up to the front door and I kept pace with him. If anything, I was more excited than frightened. It was Laura who was hanging back a little. This was as unusual as her being quiet and, once again, I wondered what was wrong with her.

'OK,' Dad said when we were standing on the top step, the bulk of the house looming over us. 'Alistair was supposed to come up to the house and knock on the door. What was it you told him to shout?'

'Gerald Manson. I've come to visit you.'

I felt a right twerp saying this. PC Wren must have agreed with me because I noticed he was smirking as he watched Dad take hold of the big metal knocker. When Dad did something, he did it well. He banged that knocker so hard I was surprised some of the loose slates didn't fall off the roof.

'Gerald Manson,' he shouted. 'This is Inspector Venables. I've come to pay you a visit.'

For a moment or two afterwards there was silence. Although a couple of birds flew out of one of the trees, nothing moved inside the house. This made me very glad. Even with Dad beside me, I wasn't quite sure what I'd have done if something had answered the door.

'It doesn't look as though Gerald is at home, Constable,' Dad said with a laugh.

'It doesn't look like it, sir,' PC Wren agreed.

He stepped forward and tried the door but it was locked. Dad had gone over to one of the windows beside the door and was peering inside, using one hand to shield the light from his eyes. After a few seconds he went to the window on the other side of the door and did the same.

'Alistair certainly didn't go in here,' he said when he finally stood back. 'That dust hasn't been disturbed for years. All the same, Constable, you'd better check the rest of the downstairs windows, just to make sure.'

'All right, sir.'

PC Wren went off and Dad started poking around among the weeds growing in the drive in front of the house. Once he'd explained what he was doing, Laura and I joined in. Although we found a couple of places where the weeds looked as though they'd been squashed flat by a bicycle tyre, this wasn't a great deal of help. We already knew Alistair had been there with his bicycle the previous night.

PC Wren hadn't done any better on his trip round the house. All the windows and doors were firmly secured, so there was no way Alistair could have got inside. In any case, there wasn't a single footprint to be seen in the thick dust. As far as he was concerned, it was pretty obvious. Ali hadn't been into the Manson house.

'Right,' Dad said to the constable. 'I think that just about wraps it up. When we get back to the station, you can grab young Hendricks. The two of you had better check the grounds, just to make sure there isn't

50

anything we missed, but don't waste too much time on it. There are other things to do.'

'Aren't you going to look inside the house?' I found this hard to believe. I mean, I didn't want to go inside myself, but I thought somebody ought to check.

'What's the point, Tom? There's no way Alistair could have got in and, even if he had, there would have been footprints all over the place.'

'He could have been grabbed and carried inside.' Although I could feel my face going red, I'd had to say it.

'In that case, whoever carried him inside would have left footprints.'

'Not necessarily.'

For a second or two Dad just stood and looked at me.

'You're still thinking about ghosts and evil spirits, are you?' he asked.

'Yes.'

At times I have a very stubborn streak. Although I knew how stupid I must sound, I couldn't let it go. At least Dad didn't laugh out loud, however amused he might have been inside.

'Tell me something, Tom,' he said. 'Have you ever heard of a ghost riding a bicycle.'

'Of course I haven't.'

Now I was puzzled. I didn't have the slightest idea what Dad was talking about.

'Nor have I, but somebody rode Alistair's bike. It was found outside the station at Overthorpe this morning.'

'What would it be doing there?' By now I was confused as well.

'I wish we knew. The only thing we can think of is

51

that there are all-night trains from Overthorpe to London. That's where Alistair used to live, and both his parents said he hadn't settled down very well here in Wroxford. He hadn't made many friends and he was always talking about how he missed his old neighbourhood.'

It was as though a great weight had been lifted from my shoulders. I'd been sure something terrible had happened to Ali because of our stupid dare, and this was one occasion when I was happy to be proved wrong. I mean, I'd been imagining old Gerald Manson's ghost capturing Ali and doing horrible things to him. The thought of some evil spirit doing this and then pedalling the five miles to Overthorpe was simply too silly for words. If Ali's bike was in Overthorpe, this was where he must have gone after he'd left us. The reason why didn't matter so much. It was just nice to know I wasn't responsible for whatever had happened.

Although it was probably very selfish of me, considering Ali was still missing, the thought cheered me up all the way back to school. If it was cheering Laura up, she was hiding it pretty well. She was as silent as she'd been all morning and I didn't get a chance to speak to her alone until after we'd been dropped back at school.

'Aren't you pleased?' I asked as we went through the main entrance.

'What about?'

'That whatever happened to Ali isn't our fault.'

'How do we know that?'

This was Laura doing her Mary, Mary, quite contrary, bit. Earlier on she'd been convinced that nothing had happened to Ali at the Manson house.

Now Dad had proved she was right, she seemed to have changed her mind. That's girls for you.

'For goodness sake,' I said. 'What's bothering you now?'

'The gate,' she answered.

I didn't have any idea what she was talking about and, as we'd reached the door of the classroom, there was no chance to ask her. In any case, I didn't let it bother me for too long. I was too happy to be off the hook.

5

Ali still hadn't turned up by the Thursday night. Both Laura and me were waiting for Dad when he came home from work but he had nothing new to tell us. Apparently we were still the last people to have seen Ali. Nobody had come forward to say they'd seen him cycling to Overthorpe. Nobody remembered him getting on a train. Although he didn't actually say so, I could tell Dad was becoming increasingly worried. So was Laura. At least, I assumed this was what was bugging her, because she wasn't talking. After tea she went up to her room and she didn't come down again. I did stick my head around the door a couple of times but she said she was busy with her homework, so I left her alone.

The next morning she was even worse. She hardly said a word on the way to school and in class she was almost in a trance. Normally, hers is one of the first hands which go up when Mr Langley asks a question. Today she didn't move, not even when he asked her something directly.

'I don't think she's with us today,' he said, and a little titter ran round the class. 'Are you all right, Laura?'

This time the mention of her name made her give a little start. I could tell she hadn't heard anything that had gone before.

'I'm sorry, sir. What did you say?'

'I asked if you were all right.'

For a second Laura just sat there. Then she shook her head.

'No, sir, I'm not. I feel sick.'

She was so pale, she really did look ill. Mr Langley must have thought so too. He not only told her to go to the medical room, he let me go with her.

'What is it?' I asked, once we were in the corridor. 'Are you still bothered about Ali?'

'Aren't you, Tom?' Her voice was almost fierce.

'Of course I am, but I'm not making myself sick over it. It's not our fault he went to Overthorpe and disappeared.'

'What makes you so sure he went to Overthorpe?' Laura had grabbed hold of my arm to stop me walking any further and her eyes were almost feverish.

'His bike was found there,' I pointed out.

'I know, and that doesn't make sense. Did we imagine what we saw and heard at the Manson house last Sunday?'

'You know we didn't.'

Despite myself, I couldn't suppress a shiver.

'It was Hallowe'en, too, the night when Alistair disappeared. That's when terrible things are supposed to happen up there.'

'But they didn't to Ali. He was fit enough to cycle to Overthorpe.'

'How do we know that?'

Laura had started walking again and I had to run a few paces to catch up.

'Because his bike was there,' I told her. 'How do you explain that?'

'I can't.' Laura made no bones about it. 'You explain one thing to me, though. How do you account for the gate?'

'What about the gate?'

This was the second time Laura had mentioned it and I still didn't know what she was talking about.

'We left it open on Sunday,' Laura explained, 'but when we went up there with Alistair it was closed. He left it open too, and when we went to the Manson house with Dad it was shut again. How do you account for that?'

'It was probably the wind.'

'I don't think so,' Laura said. 'Any more than I think Alistair ever left the Manson house.'

I'd have liked the chance to tell Laura she was crazy, that bikes don't pedal themselves, but I didn't have the chance. We'd reached the door of the medical room and this was where I had to leave her.

'She's cracking up,' I muttered to myself as I started to walk back to class.

The trouble was, I couldn't completely convince myself. Crazy or not, Laura had planted a little seed of doubt at the back of my mind.

At lunchtime I went to see old Max. He was in one of his chatty moods and it was no great trick to steer the conversation in the direction of the Manson house. This is an area where he is an authority, and he loves nothing more than an appreciative audience. In fact, once he started, it was difficult to get a word in edgeways. Not that this bothered me. Max was pretty interesting anyway, and he was saying something I wanted to hear. According to him, there had probably been countless deaths and tragedies up at the house. Everybody knew about the Gerald Manson massacre and the girl in the garden, but there had been plenty of mysterious disappearances in Wroxford over the years, people who had left home never to return, and in a lot of cases no trace of them had ever been discovered. There had been no bodies and no clues as to where the missing persons had gone. Old Max didn't have any doubts as to what had happened. The Manson house had claimed them.

All this talk of mysterious disappearances had the icy fingers walking up and down my spine again. Although Ali's name hadn't been mentioned, this was who I was thinking of. If Laura had planted the seed earlier, old Max was helping it to grow. I mean, it was very convenient for me to assume Ali had cycled to Overthorpe, because this let me off the hook. All the same, there was no denying the fact that the Manson house was the last place where Ali had been seen.

'Tell me something, Max.' He'd stopped talking to take a quick slurp of tea and I seized my opportunity. 'Last time I was here, you were saying the Manson house was an evil place. What did you mean?'

'Just what I said, Thomas. There are places where evil flourishes, and that's one of them.'

'So it's the house that's evil, not what's inside?'

By now the icy fingers were doing a tap dance.

'Oh no, Thomas.' Max was shaking his bald head. 'It's the place itself. Hundreds of years ago Runton Hill was a meeting place for the Druids. Unspeakable things they used to do up there, unspeakable. There used to be human sacrifices, the lot.'

'You mean bad things have always happened up there?'

'Not quite.' Old Max was warming to his theme as he poured himself another cup of tea. 'For a long time

57

the hill was quiet but the evil was always there, buried, deep down under the ground. It was biding its time, waiting to be released. If you check the records, you'll probably find the disappearances didn't start until after the house was built.'

'It was the builders who did it then?' My voice had almost dropped to a whisper.

'It was Wilberforce Manson tampering with nature,' Max said darkly. 'The house itself couldn't have caused too much harm. The foundations wouldn't have been deep enough to release the horrors which were waiting in the hill.'

'What did this Wilberforce Manson do?'

'He dug, Thomas, just as he'd been doing all his life. Wilberforce was the first of the Mansons to settle here in Wroxford. He was the one who started the paper mill. Before that, though, he'd been a tin miner in Cornwall. Digging down into the ground was in his blood.'

'What would he mine around here?'

'It wasn't a mine he dug, it was a tunnel. When the house was finished he brought some of his friends up from Cornwall. They stayed at the house while they were digging the tunnel. It was supposed to go all the way from the house into Wroxford and they dug right down into the hill. It was never quite completed, though.'

'Why was that?' I asked.

'Who knows?' Old Max shrugged and slurped some more tea. 'One day Wilberforce's Cornish friends just upped and went. Rumour has it that not nearly so many returned to Cornwall as originally came. I'd say the hill was hungry after its long rest. Those miners would have been its first victims after it woke up.'

Just then the bell began ringing and I had to leave. All the same, old Max had given me plenty of new material for nightmares. Although I wasn't entirely sure what a Druid was, I'd understood all about the human sacrifice bit. It helped to bring out something which had already been there at the back of my mind. The one sure way for Ali to have disappeared so completely was for him to be dead.

I was watching 'Scooby Doo' on television when Laura wandered in and dumped herself on the sofa. Usually the cartoon made me laugh like a drain, but tonight I hadn't even managed a smile. Somehow I wasn't finding ghosts and haunted houses very funny any more. This was why I didn't complain when Laura used the remote control to switch it off.

'I want to talk to you, Tom.'

'That makes a change.'

The sarcasm was wasted. All Laura was thinking about was what she wanted to say.

'I've got to do something about Alistair,' she went on. 'Whatever happened to him is all my fault.'

'Not all,' I pointed out. 'I've got a share of it too. The trouble is, there's nothing we can do. Dad and the police are already doing everything that's possible. If they can't find Ali, we're not likely to do any better.'

'I'm not so sure, Tom.' Although Laura was no crybaby, I could sense she was on the verge of tears. 'Dad and the police aren't looking in the right place.'

'You're talking about the Manson house again?'

'You know I am. That's where it happened, Tom, not in Overthorpe or London or anywhere else. I'm sure of it.'

So was I now, but I still didn't see what I could do.

'The police have already been there,' I told her. 'If you remember, we were there with them. They didn't find anything at all.'

'They only looked in the grounds, Tom. They didn't go inside the house.'

'What do you mean?'

The trouble was, I knew exactly what she meant. The very thought of what Laura was about to suggest made me go cold inside.

'It's Saturday tomorrow.' Laura seemed to be talking from a long way away. 'I'm going up to the Manson house to see if I can find a way inside.'

'You're crazy.'

I'd never meant anything more.

'Maybe I am but I have to do it.'

'Aren't you scared?'

'Of course I am. I'm petrified, but it still has to be done. And I want you to come with me.'

'No way, Laura.'

I meant this even more.

'It's all right, Tom, I'm not asking you to come inside. All I want you to do is wait by the gate. If I'm gone for more than half an hour, you can go and fetch help.'

As I sat there looking at my sister, I could feel the love and pride growing inside me. She was so brave; much, much braver than I could ever be, even if she was crazy. I mean, I only had to look at her white, pinched face to see how frightened she was, but she'd still force herself to do it.

'It isn't going to help Ali if you disappear too,' I said.

'I don't think I will. It will be daylight when I go up there and it isn't Hallowe'en.'

'All the same, there must be a better way.'

'Such as?'

'We could get Dad to take a look around inside.'

'How? He doesn't believe the Manson house is haunted. As far as he's concerned, Alistair disappeared in Overthorpe.'

'Leave it to me,' I said, speaking with a lot more confidence than I felt. 'I'll persuade him.'

Somehow. I had to, if only to keep Laura safe.

When Dad gets home from work, he likes to sit down with a beer and watch the six o'clock news on BBC. I waited until both were finished before I spoke to him.

'Can I have a word with you, Dad?' I asked.

'Of course you can, son. I was wondering what the matter with you was. The way you've been wriggling around for the last ten minutes, I thought you wanted to go to the toilet.'

'Can we talk in private?'

'Sure, if that's what you want.'

Dad gave Mum a big wink and followed me through into the kitchen.

'So, what do you want to talk about?' he asked, once we were both sitting at the table.

'Ali Barber,' I told him.

'I'm afraid there's not much more I can tell you except that he hasn't been found yet. I'm not on the case any more.'

'Why ever not?'

There was a sinking sensation in my stomach.

'Us police inspectors are far too important to spend all our time looking for missing boys.' Dad was smiling to let me know he didn't really think he was very important at all. 'Besides, we've heard rumours that a particularly nasty bunch of villains has moved into our patch. We don't want them lifting any payrolls in Wroxford.'

'Ali might be dead.'

There was a long pause before Dad nodded his head.

'That is a possibility,' he agreed, 'but there's no evidence to suggest it. If there was, Alistair's disappearance would take priority over everything else. As it is, there are a lot of policemen trying to find him in both Overthorpe and London.'

'They're searching in the wrong place, Dad. They should be looking up at the Manson house. That's where it happened.'

'What happened?'

'I don't know exactly,' I said miserably. 'It must have been terrible though.'

'You're still thinking about those ghosties and ghoulies, are you?'

'Yes, and so is Laura.'

There was a defiant tone in my voice which made Dad nod his head again. He might not have believed what I was saying but at least he wasn't dismissing it out of hand.

'Do you know something, Tom,' he said. 'I've been a policeman for over twenty years and there's never been a ghost involved in a single case I've handled.'

'There's a first time for everything,' I pointed out. 'Besides, Laura and me have seen them.'

'What do you mean?'

So I told him about our conkering expedition and what we'd seen and heard. When I'd finished, Dad called Laura in. She told him pretty much the same, only a little bit better. She had a way with words that I didn't.

'OK,' Dad said, when we'd both had our say. 'You still don't have me thinking ghosts because I don't believe there are such things. You two obviously do, though. What would you like me to do to put your minds at rest?'

'Have a look inside the Manson house.' Laura spoke without any hesitation.

'All right. That should be easy enough to fix, especially if it's going to earn me some peace from you two. I'll arrange it for first thing in the morning, but there's one condition. I want both of you to come with me when I go.'

Although I couldn't pretend either of us was bursting with enthusiasm, neither of us raised any objections. It was an awful lot better going to the Manson house with Dad than it would have been going on our own.

'Are you two frightened?' Dad asked.

'Yes.'

This was from Laura. I simply nodded my head. We had collected the key from Mr Pettigrew at the local estate agent's and now we were standing at the bottom of the crumbling front steps, looking up at the front door of the Manson house. It was a gloomy, overcast day. This was more or less the way I felt, gloomy and a little bit apprehensive. For once, Dad's presence wasn't as reassuring as usual. I wasn't entirely certain how he'd measure up to a ghost.

'Don't worry, you two.' Dad was trying the jovial bit to snap us out of our mood. 'It's the spectres and spooks that need to watch out. You probably didn't know it, but I'm an honorary member of Ghost-busters.'

'That isn't funny, Dad,' Laura told him.

'Let me put it another way then. I've brought my personal radio with me. If we do bump into anything, I can have all the Wroxford police force up here in a couple of minutes. Does that make you feel any better?'

Although we both agreed it did, I think we were both lying. I know I was. A couple of minutes would seem an awful long time if we bumped into Gerald Manson or some of the Druids.

'Here's what we do,' Dad went on. 'When we go inside, we stick together and we go through every room in turn. You've both brought your torches, haven't you?'

We had, but Laura wasn't ready to go inside the Manson house yet.

'Can we have a walk round the outside first?'

'What are you doing?' Dad asked. 'Trying to postpone the evil moment?'

'Something like that.'

We all walked slowly round the house. I wasn't sure what Laura was looking for, but whatever it was, this was OK with me. Even with Dad there, it was going to take a lot of courage for me to step into the house. I couldn't help remembering all that Max had told me, and the shadow I'd seen at the window.

All too soon we were back where we'd started and Dad was putting the big, old-fashioned key into the lock. To my surprise, the door didn't creak at all when it was opened. Dad was surprised too.

'They don't make locks like that any more,' he

said, pulling the key out and examining it. 'I was half expecting it to be jammed solid. Anyway, torches at the ready.'

The door might not have creaked but the entrance hall we went into was like the set of a horror movie — and it wasn't just the thick carpet of dust on the floor. There were cobwebs everywhere and the furniture was covered with sheets. Sheets made me think of ghosts and I started to shiver. When something moved in the darkness beyond the beams of our torches, making a faint, scuttling sound, I jumped a mile. So did Laura, because she was suddenly holding on to Dad's other arm.

'Calm down,' he said, playing his flashlight around the mildewed portraits which still hung on the walls. 'It was only a mouse. Which way do you want to go first?'

'Left,' Laura told him.

'Right,' I said at the same instant.

'It's good to see you're both in agreement. Let's compromise. We'll go straight ahead.'

Straight ahead meant up the wide staircase, and neither of us argued. Dad had already started walking forward, and wherever he went, we were going too. When it came to creaking, the stairs more than made up for the front door. All the steps seemed to be loose and, with three of us going up at the same time, it was like some hideous orchestra. The higher we went, the bigger the cobwebs became, some of them hanging down from the ceiling to brush against our faces. This started me wondering about the size of the creatures which had made them. I mean, I knew what a normal web looked like and some of those I could see in the torchlight were forty or fifty times larger. If the spiders which had spun them were that much bigger as well, I certainly didn't want to meet them. They'd be large enough to take out for a walk on a lead.

When Dad stopped on the landing, I had something new to worry about. The landing was where Mrs Manson had been shot, and this probably meant it was a very bad place to be.

'What are we waiting for?' I whispered.

'I'm a bit worried about the floor up here.' Dad insisted on talking in a normal voice. I wanted to tell him to be a bit quieter because I didn't want anything to hear us. 'You'd better take the lead, Tom.'

'Me?' I squeaked.

'You're lighter than I am,' Dad explained. 'If the floor is a bit rotten, you're less likely to go through.'

This was really terrific. Now I didn't just have ghosts and man-eating spiders to worry about. At any moment I was likely to go plunging through the floorboards. I started off as though I was walking on eggs, with Dad giving me the occasional little push from behind to keep me moving, but the floor seemed safe enough. Each door we came to, we pushed open and shone our torches inside. There was no need to go in because it was obvious nobody had been there for years. Nobody human, at any rate. There was dust all over the floor and furniture and it was undisturbed apart from the tracks of the mice.

The longer we were, the more nervous I became. Apart from the noise we made, the house was almost oppressively quiet. All the same, I had the growing feeling there was someone or something with us, and I wasn't thinking of mice. I had the feeling I was being watched and observed, and Laura felt the same. Although she didn't say anything, she was like me. Several times we turned to flash our torches behind us, just to make sure there wasn't anything there in the darkness. My heart wasn't exactly in my mouth but I had a nasty sick taste there. All I wanted to do was get out in the fresh air again.

The last room we came to upstairs had been the nursery. Toys with most of their stuffing chewed out by the mice lay on the floor, and what once had been a muslin cover hung in tatters over the bed. This was another bad place, the room where the two Manson children had been murdered. I stayed well back in the doorway beside Dad, but after a moment's hesitation, Laura went inside. She picked her way across the room and stood by the window.

'What are you doing?' I asked. My voice was still a whisper.

'Just looking,' she said, walking back towards us.

Normally I would have been curious to know what she was looking for or at, but not now. All I wanted was to get away from the nursery, down the stairs and out of the house. Although we managed the first two smartly enough, we still had the downstairs rooms to go through. Once we were down at ground level again, Dad took over the lead and this made me feel slightly better. Not much, though. I couldn't rid myself of the feeling that something was keeping an eye on our every step, watching to make sure we didn't uncover whatever secrets the house might hide. Fortunately, we didn't and, after what seemed like an eternity, we were standing on the steps while Dad relocked the front door. It was still as gloomy as ever, with a light drizzle falling, but I'd never been quite so glad to be out in the open. I was breathing easily for the first time since we'd arrived at the Manson house.

'OK, you two,' Dad said. 'Are we all agreed that there weren't any signs of Alistair ever having been in the house?'

'Yes, Dad,' Laura and me chorused together.

'Did either of you see any ghosts, ghouls, spectres, spooks, blobs of ectoplasm or anything super-natural?'

'No, Dad.'

'In that case, let's hope you've got it all out of your system and can leave me in peace. Come on. Let's take the key back to Mr Pettigrew, then go and have some lunch.'

Laura and me went without any argument. All the same, I couldn't say I *had* got the Manson house out of my system. Although there hadn't been any signs of Ali, I was more convinced than ever that there was something wrong with the place. Laura felt the same. She made this pretty plain after we were back home and Dad had gone to join Mum in the kitchen.

'The gate was shut again,' she said.

'I noticed.'

'It makes you wonder who keeps closing it, doesn't it?'

'Or what.'

I'd had a good look at the gate when we went in and the wind couldn't possibly have blown it shut. The hinges were starting to go and the bottom of the gate scraped along the ground when it was pushed open.

'Alistair didn't go out of the other gate,' she went on.

'How do you know?'

'The path was completely overgrown. There's no way he could have got through, especially in the dark.'

Now Laura mentioned it, this was something else I'd noticed. The path was completely covered with thistles and willowherb and the like, most of it well above my head. Even if Ali had been able to force his way through, there would have been some marks of his passage. You didn't need to be a detective to see nobody had been that way for years. All the same, I didn't make any comment because I didn't want to encourage Laura. I could see the direction the conversation was going and it was somewhere I didn't want to travel.

'We didn't find that tunnel old Max told you about, either. There was no sign of it anywhere.'

'Perhaps it's been blocked up.'

'Maybe, but there's another thing as well.' Once Laura had her teeth into something, she didn't let go easily. 'I found a way to get inside the house.'

'So did I,' I said. 'You borrow the key from the estate agent's and go in through the front door.'

'Ha, ha, ha.' Laura wasn't exactly overwhelmed by my wit. 'That wasn't what I meant and you know it. You can get in through the nursery window — the catch is loose and it doesn't close properly. All you have to do is climb on to the roof of the garage and step inside.'

'Terrific,' I said. 'Perhaps you can lay on a guided tour for next Hallowe'en. If you do, count me out. I've seen all I ever want to see of the Manson house.'

The trouble was, wanting wasn't enough. There

was an invisible thread linking me to the Manson house, and wishes weren't enough to break it.

6

All my friends were out, apart from Darren Inglis — and he was no good to man or beast. He'd been caught scrumping apples from his neighbours' garden for the umpteenth time, which meant he was grounded for the weekend. In the half an hour I'd been away from home, Dad and Laura had gone out and Mum was putting on her warpaint. This was a sure sign she was off out as well.

'It's the Babes in the Wood in reverse,' I said gloomily.

'What is, dear?'

'Me being abandoned by everybody. Am I really that objectionable?'

'Yes, you are,' Mum said comfortingly, applying a last dab of lipstick. 'But we may come back eventually when it turns cold.'

'Great. Where is everybody.'

'I'm here wasting time talking to you when there's shopping to be done. Dad has gone into the station.'

'How about Laura?'

'Your guess is as good as mine, Tom. She's gone out somewhere on her bike.'

'Great,' I said again. 'There is one thing about it, though. If I'm ever put into prison, I'll already be used to solitary confinement.'

'You'll also be expected to keep your cell tidy,' Mum pointed out. 'Since you're obviously at a loose end, you can spend the afternoon putting your room straight. It looks like a rubbish tip.'

This was probably a bit unfair to rubbish tips. I mean, my room usually looks a mess, but what Mum doesn't understand is that there's a system behind it. It's my stuff and I know exactly where everything is. There are an awful lot of things I use in the course of a week, and it is handy to have them where I can get at them instead of having to hunt through cupboards and wardrobes. This was an argument I'd tried with Mum before. As usual, it didn't work, so I went upstairs to do as she'd said. It was a good thing I did. Otherwise I might not have found the note Laura had left on my bed. She'd written it in block capitals. TOM, it said, I'M GOING BACK TO THE MANSON HOUSE TO TRY TO FIND THE TUNNEL. IF ANYTHING HAPPENS TO ME YOU'D BETTER TELL MUM AND DAD.

I'd have liked to tell Mum or Dad immediately. Unfortunately, I couldn't. Mum had already left, and when I rang the police station, Dad wasn't there. For a minute or two I dithered, wondering what to do for the best. Should I stay at home until Mum or Dad came back? Should I go and tell one of the neighbours? Better still, should I ring the police station again and tell the officer on duty?

When I thought about them, none of these were very good ideas. Mum and Dad might be a long time, and what could I tell the police or the neighbours? Laura had been gone for less than an hour and, however dangerous the Manson house might be in my mind, most grown-ups would be as unconvinced as Dad. The only person I knew who was likely to believe me was old Max, and there was no way I could contact him. Saturday afternoons he went into Norwich to watch the Canaries play.

If anybody was going to help Laura, it had to be me. All the same, it didn't make sense for me to go to the Manson house as well. Or was I just making excuses for doing nothing because I was scared? Although I hadn't thought about this before, I did now; and the more I thought, the more uneasy I became. Whatever Dad thought, I was like Laura. I knew that whatever had caused Ali to disappear had happened at the Manson house. There was no real doubt in my mind at all. This meant it was partly my fault, because Laura and me had taken him there. It was my responsibility to try to help him if it wasn't already too late. This was something Laura had realized all along. I'd kept it hidden from myself because I wasn't as brave as she was.

'Right, Venables,' I muttered. 'Let's see what you're made of.'

It was mostly quaking jelly, but this didn't stop me going to the garage to collect my bike.

All the way up Runton Hill I kept hoping I'd meet Laura coming the other way, but I didn't. The first sign of her was her bike, in the hedge about a hundred metres from the gates of the Manson house. Part of me insisted that this was where I ought to stay too. I could wait to see if Laura came out, and if she didn't, I could fetch help. Appealing though the idea was, I tried not to listen to it. I knew this was a test for me. Laura had gone inside to see if she could do anything for Ali and I had to do the same. I couldn't be a coward all my life.

'Come on,' I told myself. 'You went into the house this morning. Nothing happened then.'

'But Dad was there to look after you,' the cowardly part of me answered. 'And you were scared stiff even then.'

The cowardly part of me was winning the argument hands down, so I put an end to it. I was going into the garden, and if I didn't find Laura there, I was going into the house. This was all there was to it. Besides, I had protection. Mum's big old crucifix had been banging against my chest all the way up the hill and now I pulled it out of the top of my sweater, clutching it tightly in one hand. In most of the horror films I'd seen, you only had to hold a crucifix to protect yourself against evil. Mind you, there were a few where it had been no protection at all, but I preferred not to think about them.

The gate was open for once, and I went through before I could dream up any more reasons not to. The gravel crunched under my feet and the noise made me uncomfortable, so I moved on to the grass verge, right under the trees. Although the cowardly me was screaming that I should go back while I still could, I refused to listen. In some ways it was easier than I'd expected. Frightened as I was, my legs still worked, so it was simply a question of taking one step after another. There were a couple of occasions when I thought I heard something moving in the trees to my right, but I kept going, clutching the crucifix. Once I could see the house ahead of me, I squeezed so hard it was cutting into my flesh. In my imagination, the windows were eyes, watching me come closer and closer. The house was waiting for me, I was another victim. For a moment I faltered. Somehow, though, I forced myself on, keeping to the grass verge until I was standing beside the garage.

Laura was right. Now I was looking, I could see how easy it was to climb on to the roof of the garage. There was one of those old-fashioned drainpipes and the pieces of metal attaching it to the wall were like a ladder. It was almost too easy. It was as though the house was inviting me inside, and the thought made me shudder. All the same, I started climbing. Now I'd come so far, I might as well go the whole way.

It was the final step which was the most difficult. I'd climbed up the drainpipe; I was on the garage roof. All I had to do was pull open the nursery window and I'd be inside. The trouble was, I didn't want to. My yellow streak had resurfaced and it was reminding me of all the dreadful things which might be waiting for me inside. To fill in time, I tried peering through the window. This wasn't a great deal of help. Even with the afternoon light behind me, all I could see was the bed and the rest of the furniture. With the door leading to the corridor closed, most of the room was in darkness and I couldn't distinguish much more than outlines.

In the end, it was the ribbon which persuaded me inside. It was blue and white candy-striped and, the last time I'd seen it, the ribbon had been on Laura's ponytail. Now it was tied to the handle on the inside of the window. I knew exactly why it was there. If anything did happen to her, Laura didn't want there to be any mistake. She wanted everybody to know it had happened inside the Manson house.

Opening the window was as easy as climbing up the drainpipe had been. Although the catch was down, the window was so loose in the frame, I only had to jiggle it a bit before it came open. After this it was a question of taking a deep breath, saying a quick prayer and switching on the torch before I climbed over the sill. My heart was pounding away in my chest as though it wanted to break out, and as soon as both my feet were on the mouldy carpet, I clutched the crucifix in my free hand. Frightened as I was, I felt proud as well. I mean, I'd actually done it. I'd gone into the Manson house on my own and I wasn't going to turn back now.

Walking on tiptoe, I followed Laura's footsteps across the floor. When I reached the door, I put my ear against the wood and listened. At first there was nothing to hear. The house was completely silent around me. 'Deathly quiet' was the phrase which popped into my mind, and this made me shiver. This was when I heard the faint scraping sound. It was difficult to tell where it came from or what might have caused it. I pressed my ear even closer to the door, but this was a waste of time. The second time I heard the noise, I knew exactly where it had come from. It was coming from behind me. There was something in the room with me.

'It's a mouse,' I said, desperately trying to convince myself.

I knew I was lying. I'd heard mice scurrying around earlier in the day and they'd made a very different sound from the scraping noise I could hear behind me now. This was made by something much, much bigger and almost certainly far, far more dangerous. While I was thinking this, I was swinging round so fast that my hand banged against the chest of drawers beside the door and I dropped my torch.

As it hit the floor, there was a crack of breaking glass and the light went out. I would have screamed then if I'd been able to, but all the muscles in my body were frozen with terror.

Even in the semidarkness, I knew just where the noise was coming from. It was coming from the bed, the very bed where two children had been murdered in their sleep. Now there was something under the bed and it was coming out to get me. I could see the covers moving and bulging as the thing struggled to free itself. Eyes bulging out of my head with fright, I watched as a white skeletal hand appeared and began inching across the floor towards me. Then a second hand appeared and I couldn't take any more. I closed my eyes, clutched the crucifix in both hands and started praying as I'd never prayed before.

'Our Father which art in Heaven,' I gabbled, 'Hallowed be Thy name.'

But it wasn't working. I could hear the thing squeezing itself out from beneath the bed and oozing across the floor towards me. My legs suddenly came unhinged at the knees and I slid down the wall, ending up on the floor in a quivering heap, still praying away like mad.

'Tom,' the thing whispered. 'Tom. That is you, isn't it?'

For a dreadful moment my heart stopped completely. Then it started pumping again and I was furiously angry. The 'thing' had a voice I recognized.

'You silly little cow,' I hissed. 'What do you think you were doing under there? You nearly gave me a heart attack.'

Furious as I was, I still remembered to whisper.

'I was hiding,' Laura told me. 'I didn't know who was coming in the window, did I?'

I was going to say that if there was anything to be afraid of, it was inside the house, not coming through the window, but I managed to stop myself. I was inside too and I didn't want to think about what might be sharing the house with us. In any case, Laura was right. I'd have dived under the bed if I'd heard somebody climbing in through the window. The only reason I'd been angry was because she'd frightened me so much.

'Can we go now?' I asked.

'We've only just got here.'

'I've only just got here,' I pointed out. 'You must have been here hours.'

'This was as far as I'd got, Tom. I was too scared to open the door into the corridor.'

This made me feel slightly better. It also gave me a chance to show off a little. Once I was up off the floor, I threw open the door as if I didn't have a care in the world. Not that this helped a great deal. It was really dark outside and my torch wasn't working at all. Laura's was, though. When she came across to join me, I could see the same dust and cobwebs I'd seen that morning.

'Look, Tom,' Laura hissed in my ear.

'What?' I squeaked.

I couldn't have jumped more than three metres in the air. Perhaps she really was trying to give me a heart attack.

'The dust. Look at the dust.'

'What do you want me to do about it? Start spring-cleaning?'

'Of course not, you idiot. There aren't any footprints.'

Laura was right, and all of a sudden the hairs on the back of my neck were standing up like the hackles of an angry dog. Earlier in the day three of us had walked up and down the corridor, but now all our footprints had gone. It didn't make any kind of sense. I mean, I could understand why humans wanted to clear dust up, but why would ghosts want to do the opposite? One thing was sure, though. Someone or something had been upstairs since we had left.

'There's something very strange here.' Laura sounded more excited than frightened. 'Why would ghosts want to spread dust around?'

'I don't know. Perhaps it makes them feel more comfortable. I'll ask next time I meet one.' This was likely to be very soon the way Laura was waving her torch around. 'Come on. Let's get out of here.'

'Not yet. We haven't found the tunnel. Where do you think it is?'

'Well it's hardly likely to be upstairs.'

'I know that, idiot. What I meant was that we opened every door in the house and we didn't find a cellar. There must be a trap door somewhere.'

'All the downstairs floors had carpets on them.'

And there was lots of heavy furniture standing on the carpets.

'Not all of them.' Laura was sounding excited again. 'There were floorboards in the kitchen. I know because I noticed. I'm going downstairs to take a look. You'd better stay up here, just in case you need to go for help.'

'You're crazy,' I said. 'A moment ago you were too

scared to open a door. Now you're talking about marching all over the house.'

'I know,' Laura told me, 'but it's different now. I feel safer with you here, Tom.'

This was just about the nicest thing anybody had ever said to me. It made me feel good all the while Laura was walking along the corridor. It wasn't until she reached the landing at the end that I suddenly realized something. I didn't feel at all safer with me there in the Manson house.

While Laura was on the stairs, I could see the reflected beam of her torch making strange shadows on the walls. Then she must have gone into one of the downstairs rooms because everything was dark again. I stood there in the nursery doorway, listening to the small noises of the house around me and wishing I was somewhere else. The more I thought about the reappearing dust, the more it worried me. It was yet another example of how wrong things were at the Manson house. I couldn't stop myself thinking about what old Max had said. Perhaps dust-spreading was part of the Druids' rites.

Laura seemed to have been gone for an awfully long time, but I suspected this was simply my imagination. As I hadn't brought my watch with me, I started counting, more for something to do than anything else. It wasn't until I reached a thousand that I really began worrying. I'd been counting slowly, which meant it must have taken several minutes. Add on the minutes before I'd started counting and Laura had been gone for a considerable time. I knew exactly how far it was from the nursery to the kitchen because I'd been there in the morning.

It shouldn't have taken more than two or three minutes to get there and back. To have taken so long, Laura must have found something. Or something had found her.

A couple of seconds later I knew which it was. I'd never heard Laura scream before and it wasn't a sound I ever wanted to hear again. Although the scream only lasted for a few seconds before it was abruptly cut off, there was no mistaking the sheer terror it contained. Something had scared Laura half to death and the same something must have stopped her screaming, cutting her off in full flow.

As for me, I was my usual calm, collected self, shivering so badly I could hear the fragments of bulb rattling around in the casing of my torch. So much for Laura feeling safer with me around. I mean, there she was in mortal danger and what was I doing? It certainly wasn't anything heroic, or even useful. The best I could manage was my jelly impersonation while I dithered there in the doorway of the nursery. The trouble was, I didn't know what to do.

At least, I could think of two alternatives and I couldn't make up my mind between them. Should I go for reinforcements or should I rush downstairs to help Laura? I knew the sensible thing was to get out of the house, go back to my bike and fetch Dad and as many of the Wroxford police as he could rustle up. It was also the easy way, the cowardly way, if you like. I'd just be running away again. Laura was in trouble. Coming back with help in half an hour might not be any good at all. It might be too late for her. What Laura needed was help right now. So what, if this meant venturing down into the darkness to face the unknown danger? Laura was my twin sister and she needed me.

81

Twice I started to go out into the corridor and twice I pulled back.

The question I couldn't answer was, what was I going to do once I'd gone downstairs and found Laura? I suspected I'd be screaming too, and that wouldn't be any good to anybody.

I was still dithering when my mind was made up for me. There was a glimmer of reflected light coming from the direction of the staircase, and for one wonderful moment I thought it was Laura coming back. Only for a moment, though, until I realized the light was flickering. This wasn't a torch. It was a lamp like the one I'd seen in the window the previous Sunday. No sooner had I thought this than I saw the shadow of the figure holding the lamp — and my last hope died. The shadow wasn't Laura's. It belonged to something far larger, something which had already dealt with Laura and was now coming for me.

For the second time in a matter of minutes, I seemed to be frozen to the spot. The light became brighter and brighter as the thing came up the stairs, the shadow larger and more menacing, and still I stood there. I'd probably never have moved if one thought hadn't somehow percolated through my terror. Laura needed me. If I was caught, there'd be no one to help her at all.

With a little whimper at the back of my throat, I turned away from the doorway. Once I could no longer see the light or the shadow, the spell seemed to be broken. I was still terrified but now I was suddenly able to do what I always did when I was in danger. I ran. Six silent steps took me to the window. Another second should have seen me outside on the roof of the garage. Except that the window wouldn't open.

82

Frantic with fright, I pulled and pushed at the handle, but it wouldn't budge. The window which had opened so easily when I'd wanted to come into the Manson house had barred itself against me when I wanted to leave. It made me think of those Venus flytraps, the plants which entice insects inside, then trap them while they are eaten and digested. This was what the Manson house had done to Laura and me. Although it had welcomed us inside, it had no intention of ever allowing us to leave.

With another whimper of terror, I looked back over my shoulder. The flickering light was coming along the corridor; I could hear the slithering sound as the creature drew nearer, and I was trapped in the nursery. There was only one thing I could do. Although I didn't think this would do me any good, I did it anyway. I dived under the bed to hide in the place where Laura had hidden when she heard me coming through the window.

This didn't make me feel particularly safe. Although the covers almost reached the floor, they were very thin. I could still see the light coming nearer. It was much dimmer but I could definitely make it out. I didn't think it could see me because there weren't any lights under the bed with me. At least, that was how human eyes worked. For all I knew, the thing coming down the corridor could see right through brick walls. Besides, I had the awful feeling it knew exactly where it was going and exactly who it was looking for. I could already visualize the terrible moment when it threw back the covers and reached down to haul me out. This made me whimper again. Although it would have been much easier to scream out loud, I didn't dare make a sound. There was always a chance I was wrong. If the creature didn't know where I was, the last thing I wanted to do was give away my hiding place.

I wasn't wrong. The thing came straight down the corridor without any hesitation, not stopping until it reached the doorway of the nursery. For a second it simply stood there. The flickering light was much brighter now and I could see the shadowy outline of whatever was holding it. From where I was lying on the floor, it seemed enormous. Worse still, the creature was making little snuffling sounds as though it was actually smelling me out.

By now my heart was skittering around all over the place and I wasn't breathing at all. I'd never felt quite so helpless and alone before. All I could do to help myself was to hold Mum's crucifix out towards the door, close my eyes and pray.

Prayers weren't enough. I could hear footsteps coming into the room and they were heading directly for the bed where I was hiding. When it stopped again, the thing was right beside the bed, so close I could actually smell it. At first I couldn't identify the odour. Then I realized what it was. It was the smell of fresh, damp earth, the sort of smell you might get from something which had just climbed out of a grave. I didn't want to, but despite myself, I slowly opened my eyes. Almost immediately I wished I hadn't. The creature was even nearer than I'd thought and I could see its feet through the gap between the bottom of the covers and the floor. The snuffling sound was much louder too. It had tracked me down and now it was about to pounce.

This was when I decided I was going to scream, after all. It was the only way I had of expressing how absolutely terrified I was. My mouth was open, my neck muscles were straining, yet somehow at the very last instant I managed to hold it back. Something had just registered through my terror. The feet I was looking at were wearing trainers and above them were the bottoms of a pair of denim jeans. I mean, I'd imagined the creatures at the Manson house in all manner of shapes and guises, but I'd never imagined them in trainers and jeans. As far as I knew, they hadn't even been invented when the Druids and Gerald Manson were around. Then there was another thing. I could smell fresh earth because both trainers were covered with the stuff, and this was something else which didn't tally with what I'd been dreading. Ghosts and spirits floated around. They didn't get their feet covered with mud.

A second later I could explain the snuffling sound as well, and the last of my doubts had been dispelled.

'It's all clear upstairs.' Although I had no idea who it was talking to, the voice was thick with cold — and you couldn't get ill once you were dead. 'There's nobody else here.'

'Fine. You'd better get back down here again.'

This was no ghostly voice, either. It was somebody talking over a personal radio just like the one Dad used.

Suddenly I wasn't frightened any more. I was just angry with myself for being so stupid and behaving like some little kid. All right, the Manson house was still dangerous, but it was human danger. This was something I could understand. It was ghosts and monsters I couldn't handle.

I was thinking all this while the man was moving away from the bed, back towards the door. When I lifted the covers a little, I could see he was a big man, but no bigger than Dad, and he was wearing a check shirt. As soon as he was out of the nursery, I rolled out from under the bed. For once, I knew exactly what I was going to do. I was going to follow him downstairs and find out what had happened to Laura. After I'd made sure she was all right, I'd either rescue her myself or go to fetch help. I was done with running away.

I won't say I wasn't nervous going down the stairs, because I was. It was a different kind of nervousness, though. I was no longer expecting something hideous to jump out of the darkness at me. It was simply a matter of making sure the man who had come into the nursery didn't hear me tiptoeing down behind him.

Mind you, this was a lot easier said than done. The number of creaks there were in the stairs, I had to test every step before I put my weight on my foot. I had to be really careful, which was the same as being really slow, and by the time I reached the bottom of the stairs, the man I was following was nowhere in sight. There wasn't even the reflected glow of his lamp. For a few seconds I simply stood in the darkness, wondering where to go next. Laura had said she was going to the kitchen, and this seemed like my best bet too. The big trouble was going to be getting there. I knew the way because I'd been there in the morning, but then I'd had the light from three torches to help me. In the darkness there would be plenty of opportunities for me to lose my way. Worse still, there was plenty of furniture for me to bump into, and I couldn't afford to make any noise.

At first it wasn't too bad because there was some light coming through the windows by the front door to help me. Unfortunately, the kitchen was at the back of the house. There weren't any windows at all in the corridors I had to go along, and once I'd rounded the first corner I was in pitch-darkness. By the time I'd gone round the second, I was lost. Shuffling along the wall in the dark, it was difficult to tell how far I'd come. I already knew the little plan of the house I'd been carrying in my head must be wrong because none of the doors I'd passed seemed to match. I was beginning to be frightened again and I stopped for a few moments to calm myself down.

'Come on, Venables,' I told myself. 'Don't be a wimp all your life.'

As soon as I thought about it, the answer was obvious. All I had to do was open the next door I came to. There'd be enough light from the window for me to see where I was and I'd be able to redraw my mental plan of the Manson house.

'There you are,' I said. 'That was pretty easy wasn't it.'

I was still busy congratulating myself when I nearly broke my leg. Instead of coming down on floor, my foot stood on something round which rolled. My foot twisted away from me and I went down hard, landing on my backside with a thump which seemed to shake the house. Although both my ankle and my bottom hurt, I was far more bothered about the noise. For a long second I just sat there, holding my breath while I waited to see if I'd been heard.

When nothing happened, I began to relax again. Whatever I'd stood on was now resting beside my leg

87

and I reached down to see what it was. My hand touched smooth metal and at first I wasn't sure what it was. Then my fingers investigated further and I realized I was holding a torch. Almost at the same instant, I knew no good fairy had been along leaving me presents. It must have been Laura who dropped it.

The question was, did it still work? At least, this was the first question. The second was, did I dare switch it on to find out? I mean, if this was where Laura had dropped her torch, it was also the place where she'd been screaming. This meant the men must be somewhere nearby.

If they were, I couldn't hear them. Besides, almost anything was better than blundering around in the dark any longer. It was a lovely moment when I discovered the torch did still work. I only kept it on for a second but this was enough to show me I hadn't done badly, after all. Even if I had miscounted the doors, I was right on track because the kitchen door was there at the end of the corridor. Standing up was another relief. My backside felt a lot better and my ankle wasn't nearly as sore as I'd feared. It ached a bit but not enough to stop me walking. Or running, if it came to that.

The torch had shown there were no more obstacles ahead of me, and I walked quickly down the rest of the corridor until my hands touched the wood of the door. It was time to listen again and, as I still couldn't hear anything threatening, I used the torch a second time. There was only one thing different in the kitchen now, but it was a big difference. Laura had been absolutely right about the trap door, because a large section of the floor had been lifted up on hinges. Before I flicked the torch off again, I had a quick glimpse of steps leading down into the darkness. This was where Wilberforce Manson's tunnel had to be. It was also where I was likely to find Laura.

While I was going down the steps I had to keep the torch on, otherwise I'd probably have broken my neck. I kept it on at the bottom too because it seemed as though I'd been wrong. There wasn't anything that remotely looked like a tunnel in sight. What I was in was a cellar storeroom with no way out apart from the way I'd come in. Three walls of the room were given over to empty, dusty shelves which stretched all the way from the floor to the ceiling. The other was split up into lots of different compartments, and I guessed it was for storing bottles of wine. This wasn't too much of a guess since one old, cobwebby bottle was still in the rack. The only other thing in the cellar was really weird. I mean, nobody had done any cleaning inside the Manson house for about thirty years, but there in the middle of the cellar floor was a vacuum cleaner. It was one of those you pulled along behind you, just like the one Mum uses at home, and it just didn't make any kind of sense. The men must have brought it with them, but I couldn't begin to think why.

I didn't waste too much time wondering about it. There were far more important problems for me to solve. Old Max had told me there was a tunnel, and the cellar was the only place it could start. This had me thinking secret passages. I mean, I'd never read a book or seen a film about an old house without there being a secret passage somewhere, and I couldn't see why the Manson house should be any different. The question was, where was it? I went around the cellar, pushing and pulling everything that could be pushed or pulled, and all that happened was one of the shelves came loose and fell down. It hit the floor with such an almighty bang, I switched off the torch and scuttled to hide under the steps. After a minute or so I decided nobody else could have heard the noise. It was only then, as I was about to switch the torch back on, that I noticed the thin sliver of light shining out from beneath the wine rack. It wasn't much of a light but there was no doubt about it.

The wine rack was one of the things I'd pushed and pulled. Now I tried tapping the bottom of one of the bins and there was no mistaking the hollow sound. Unless I was completely wrong, there was no wall behind the rack and the whole thing was really some kind of door. For the moment, though, it was locked to me. Although I tried some more pushing and pulling, absolutely nothing happened.

I switched the torch back on and took another look at the wine rack. I'd been hoping I'd see a button marked PRESS or something like that but I didn't. It looked just as ordinary as it had before I'd known it was a door. The only thing about it was the single bottle of wine in one of the bins. When I reached out to take hold of it, I was vaguely thinking there might be a message inside or some instructions on the label. Although it hadn't occurred to me that the bottle itself might be the key, it was. No sooner did I have the wine bottle in my hand than the entire rack began to move away from me, swinging back on well-oiled hinges. There stretching ahead of me was the tunnel.

7

The dim light I'd seen beneath the wine rack came from an oil lamp on the wall. Twenty or thirty metres further on there was another one. Beyond that, the tunnel stretched into the distance and I guessed there would probably be more of the lamps. All the same, I wasn't very keen to go into the tunnel. It was dead straight and, as far as I could see, there was no cover at all. If I did bump into somebody coming the other way, there wouldn't be anywhere for me to hide.

On the other hand, I'd come too far to turn back now. I'd just have to hope I was lucky. Or if I wasn't, that I didn't meet anybody who could run faster than me. Keeping close to the left-hand wall, I started off, ready to turn tail at the first hint of danger. With this in mind, I hadn't made any attempt to close the wine rack behind me. If I did have to run for it, I didn't want anything blocking my way.

As it happened, I didn't have to go very far. There was a third oil lamp on the wall, just as I'd expected, and, almost opposite, there was a much larger pool of light. It took me a moment or two to realize there must be some kind of chamber or room to the side of the tunnel, and the light was coming from inside. At almost the same time, I heard the faint murmur of voices and I froze to the spot.

The voices were coming from the same place as the light, and this should have been when I turned back. Two things stopped me. The first was that I still didn't know what had happened to Laura. Second, and equally important, there were some packing cases lying on the floor at the side of the tunnel right beside the pool of light. There were big enough gaps between the cases for me to squeeze in and have somewhere to hide. If I could get to them, that is. I covered the last twenty metres on tiptoe, aware of the voices getting louder but not really listening to what they were saying. I was concentrating hard on not making any noise.

It wasn't until I'd wormed my way in among the packing cases that I began to pay attention. The first voice I heard, I recognized immediately. It belonged to the man with the cold who had come into the nursery.

'I checked everywhere,' he was saying. 'There isn't anybody else in the house.'

'You're sure of that?' The second voice belonged to an older man. 'I know how sloppy you can be.'

'I'm absolutely positive.'

'That's what I keep on saying, only nobody listens to me. I came here on my own.'

The third voice was Laura's, and just hearing her gave me a little thrill of pleasure. Although she was nervous, she didn't sound as though she was hurt. This was a great weight off my mind.

'You weren't on your own this morning,' the older man pointed out.

'That was different,' Laura told him. 'We were looking to see if our missing friend had been inside the house.'

'I still don't understand why you came back this afternoon.'

'I keep telling you, I wanted to explore properly.

Please can I go now? My mum and dad will be worrying about me.'

'I'm worrying about you.' It was still the older man doing all the talking. 'It always worries me when people tell me lies.'

'Perhaps I ought to hurt her a little.' The suggestion came from the man with the cold. 'That might persuade her to change her tune.'

I didn't know how Laura felt, but my entire body seemed to have gone icy cold. There'd been no mistaking the pleasure and anticipation in the man's voice. He wanted to hurt Laura, and if he did lay a finger on her, I'd be forced to do something — although I wasn't sure what. I couldn't just stand there.

'You heard what Sam said.' The older man was obviously talking to Laura again. 'How does that make you feel?'

'Scared,' Laura told him, and this was certainly the way she sounded. 'It won't make any difference, though. I've already told you the truth.'

'We'll soon see about that,' Sam said. 'Just leave the little brat with me for a couple of minutes.'

'No.' The older man spoke sharply and I sighed inwardly with relief. 'We've wasted enough time on her as it is. Just lock her up with the other one.'

'If you say so.' There was disappointment in Sam's voice now. 'You're the boss, Mr Manson.'

Suddenly I wasn't feeling better at all. Instead a great black wave of terror had washed over me as I realized my mistake. Ever since Sam had come into the nursery, I'd been assuming there weren't any ghosts in the Manson house after all. Now I knew better. Gerald Manson was still in residence and Sam was his human helper.

Blind terror only lasted for a few seconds before my brain started working again. I wanted to know for sure whether this Mr Manson was human or not. I mean, there was no mistaking the name Sam had used, but Mr Manson hadn't sounded at all spooky when he spoke. It hadn't even occurred to me that he might be a ghost until his name was mentioned. Then there was Laura. Although she'd been frightened, she hadn't sounded like somebody who was having a conversation with an evil spirit.

Without really thinking about it, I'd worked my way right to the end of the packing cases. This meant I was almost level with the entrance to the chamber. From his voice, I knew roughly where Manson must be, and now I started inching forward even further. Although the top half of my body was no longer hidden by the packing cases, it was the only way I'd be able to see.

It was quite a large chamber. Like the tunnel itself, the walls and rounded ceiling were roughly bricked and there were oil lamps to give light. The first thing I saw was a pile of spades, shovels and pickaxes just inside the entrance. There were also a couple of wheelbarrows. Some of the equipment was old and rusty and obviously hadn't been used for years. The rest was much newer and several of the spades still had earth on them.

So did the boots. I'd wriggled out a bit further until I could see the wooden table and a couple of chairs which were near the back of the chamber. The boots were under the table and I found them rather reassuring. Like the trainers, they didn't seem the kind of footwear a ghost would have. To make absolutely sure, I'd have to wriggle out a bit further and hope Manson wasn't looking in my direction. I was in luck because his back was to me as he sat at the table and what I could see now was even more reassuring. Like Sam, he was wearing jeans, and his tracksuit top wasn't exactly standard ghost equipment either. It seemed I could cross ghosts off my list of possible dangers again, and this didn't make me at all unhappy.

What did was the way Manson suddenly spun round, almost as though he'd sensed I was watching him. Although I shot back into the cover of the packing cases like a demented ferret, I heard his chair scrape over the floor as he pushed it back. Then I could hear his boots coming towards the entrance, heading directly for where I was. It was the nursery all over again and I cowered back into the shadows, trying to make myself as small as possible. I didn't dare look up, but when Manson stopped he was right beside the packing cases. I was sure he must be able to see me.

'What's the matter?'

I hadn't heard Sam's trainers on the packed earth of the floor but he must have come back into the chamber from wherever he'd taken Laura,

'Rats,' Manson answered. 'I've just seen one the size of a small dog.'

Although the description wasn't very flattering, I was pleased that Manson had turned away from my hiding place and gone back into the chamber.

'Horrible things,' Sam was saying. 'They give me the creeps.'

'I'm not too keen on them myself but they're the least of our worries at the moment.'

'I know,' Sam said. 'The last few days it's been like Piccadilly Circus round here. What do we do now?'

'I think we ought to pull out and lie low.'

'You mean we're giving up, Mr Manson?' Sam sounded as though he couldn't believe his ears.

'You must be joking,' Manson told him. 'Not after all the hard work we've put in. No, there's only a couple of metres to go now. We'll come back and break through on Thursday night when we do the job. Until then we steer well clear of the house.'

'What about those two kids? Do they come with us?'

'Yes.'

'Do they have to? I don't fancy child minding.'

'You won't have to. We'll dump the two of them somewhere.'

'We can't do that,' Sam objected. 'As soon as they're loose, they'll tell the police all about us.'

'Who said anything about leaving them in a condition so they can talk? I was thinking of using them as a diversion. If we dump them far enough away, the police aren't likely to come poking around here any more.'

Sam must have liked the idea because he was laughing. By contrast, I was shivering again. There was only one way I could think of to stop Laura talking.

'Do you want me to go and tell the others we're leaving?' Sam asked.

'I'll do that,' Manson told him. 'I want you to go up and check the grounds. Make absolutely certain there isn't anyone else hanging around. Collect the

96

girl's bike as well. She said she left it just outside the gate. When the rest of us are ready to leave, you can do your dust-spreading with the vacuum cleaner again.'

'OK. I'll check the grounds first.'

I hoped Sam would take his time and do it thoroughly, otherwise I was in real trouble. When Sam went to collect Laura's bike, he was going to find mine as well.

Even after Manson was out of sight, I could hear his footsteps as he went down the tunnel. I waited until they'd died away before I came out from among the packing cases. Sam had already left and I wanted to be going too, before he found my bicycle. First, though, I needed to know where Laura was.

The chamber was much larger than I'd expected. At the back, in one corner, there was what looked like the entrance to a smaller tunnel. It wasn't until I went right up to it that I realized it was simply a short passage with a door at the end. Although this had to be where Sam had taken Laura, I listened at the door, just to make sure. I could hear somebody talking inside but the door was too thick for me to distinguish what was being said. Not that this mattered, anyway. I recognized the voice and for once I was pleased to hear Ali rabbiting away nineteen to the dozen. He wouldn't have had anybody to talk at for several days and he was obviously making up for lost time. As the door was locked and there was no sign of a key, I gave a little tap. Ali stopped talking at once.

'Who is it?' The question came from Laura.

'It's me, Tom. Are you all right?'

'I'm fine.'

'I'm all right too,' Ali said. 'I told you there were no such things as ghosts.'

This was absolutely typical. I mean, there was Ali in mortal danger and he still didn't miss a chance to say 'I told you so'. I'd have liked to tell him he was in as much danger from the humans who had captured him as he would have been from any ghosts, but I didn't. Although this might have brought Ali down a peg or two, I didn't want to scare Laura.

'Can you open the door?' she asked.

'I'm afraid not,' I told her. 'One of the men must have the key.'

'You could force it open,' Ali suggested.

'It'll be faster if I go to fetch help. I'll be as quick as I can.'

'Be careful, Tom.'

'I will be.'

There was no sign of Manson returning when I reached the tunnel. This was hardly surprising if it was as long as old Max had said, stretching most of the way into Wroxford. The direction I wanted to go was clear too and I set off at a jogtrot. By now Sam should be out in the garden. It wouldn't be very long before he discovered my bike.

As soon as I was in the cellar, I switched on my torch. Although I noticed the vacuum cleaner was no longer there, it wasn't until I saw it standing beside the trap door in the kitchen that I realized what it must be used for. This solved one of the last mysteries of the Manson house. If the vacuum cleaner was fixed so it blew instead of sucked, it could be used to spread dust instead of picking it up. This would explain why there were never any footprints in the Manson house.

While I was thinking this, I kept moving and I didn't switch off the torch until I could see the front door ahead of me. It was beginning to get dark outside and very little light was coming in through the windows beside the door. Even so, I knew there would be plenty of light for Sam to see me by once I was in the garden. From now on I'd really have to watch my step.

Sam must have gone out of the front door — I could see the fresh set of footprints leading up to it — and I reckoned it would save time if I went the same way. When I tried it, the door was unlocked and I eased it open a fraction. This was going to be the most dangerous part. Once I was among the trees, I was going to be very difficult to spot. Until I'd crossed the drive, I'd be impossible to miss if Sam was anywhere around. I definitely didn't want a third body to be dumped along with Laura's and Ali's. Come to that, I didn't want any bodies to be dumped at all. It was more important than ever for me not to be caught.

There wasn't a sign of Sam when I peeped out of the door. Although this was what I'd hoped, I didn't allow it to go to my head. I knew Sam had to be out there somewhere. I only opened the door wide enough for me to slip through and I closed it carefully behind me. Thankfully, the door was still about the only thing in the house which didn't creak. For a moment, I stayed on the top step while I made another check. There was still no sign of Sam. After that, I didn't hang around. I went across the drive at a run, sprinting as hard as I could until I was among the trees on the far side. Once I was there, I felt much safer. It was so dark in the shadows, Sam was only likely to find me if he tripped over me. I decided to stay on the grass beside the drive rather than go deeper into the trees. This way I could be sure I wouldn't get lost, and it would also be considerably quicker.

Although this was probably the right decision, it wouldn't have made much difference either way. I'd only taken a couple of steps when Sam tripped over me, stepping out of the trees so close in front of me that we nearly bumped into each other. It was difficult to say which of us was more surprised, but I think it must have been Sam. At least I'd known he was out in the garden somewhere.

For a second we just stood where we were, mouths hanging open while we stared at each other. Then Sam recovered and one large hand reached out for me.

'Well, well, well,' he said with a nasty smile. 'What have we here? I think there's another one for our collection.'

'Oh no there isn't.'

I wasn't entirely sure whether I said this out loud or not. All I knew was that if Sam got his hands on me, we were finished. So I did the only thing I could. I mean, I might not be very good at football but I could still kick. My foot connected with Sam's shin so hard I could feel my toes bend. It must have hurt Sam far more because he took a step back, yelping with pain as he bent down to clutch his injured leg.

'You little beast,' he snarled, hopping around to keep his balance. 'You're going to pay for that.'

Although I was shocked by what I'd dared to do, once I'd started I decided I might as well carry on. It was the only way I could think of to stop Sam carrying out his threat. Bent over as he was, I could see the bald patch on top of his head, and this was what I aimed for with the torch, swinging my right arm as hard as I possibly could. Bits of broken glass flew everywhere, but if the torch was ruined, I hadn't done a great deal for Sam's head either. He came out with another yelp of pain and staggered to the side.

This was all I needed. Before he had a chance to recover, I was past him and sprinting, running as though my life depended on it. I knew it probably did, and this simply lent extra speed to my feet. Although I could hear Sam coming along the drive behind me, I knew he'd never catch me. If necessary, I was prepared to keep going all the way into Wroxford. I think I probably could have done, too, if I'd had the chance. I'd rounded the last bend, the gates were there ahead of me and then I tripped over one of the tussocks of grass in the drive. One instant I was running flat out. The next I was flat out, with all the wind knocked out of me. I was still down when Sam reached me.

'Right,' he snarled, grabbing hold of one arm, his fingers pinching painfully into my bicep. 'Let's be having you. I'm going to teach you a lesson you won't ever forget.'

Down in the tunnel, Manson had mistaken me for a rat. This was the way I behaved now, and a cornered rat can be very dangerous. I mean, I just didn't have anything to lose. When Sam tugged at me to get me back on my feet, I came up much faster than he'd expected, head held low so I butted him right in the middle of his big fat stomach. I must have knocked most of the air out of his lungs because he gave a gasp and released my arm. This should have been my opportunity to start running, but I couldn't.

My forehead had hit the buckle on his belt so hard I'd almost knocked myself senseless.

Some people are supposed to see stars when they bang their heads, but I saw Blackpool illuminations instead. Suddenly there were lights everywhere, and it took me a second or two to realize I wasn't imagining them. The lights were real. While I watched without understanding, people started emerging from both sides of the drive. Two of them rushed over to grab hold of Sam. Another came to me, putting his arm around my shoulders.

'Are you all right, Tom?' Dad asked.

'I don't know,' I told him. 'Tell me I'm not dreaming.'

'You're definitely not dreaming.'

'In that case I'm fine.' I'd slung both my arms around Dad by now and was hugging him close, tears prickling in my eyes. 'What are you doing here?'

'I think that's the question I should be asking you. If you remember, I'm the policeman.'

'I asked first,' I told him. Then I remembered something. 'It doesn't matter, anyway. We've got to rescue Laura.'

'Laura?' Dad had pushed me away from him, holding me at arm's length so he could see my face. 'You're not saying she's here too?'

'But she is — that's why I'm here. She's locked up in the tunnel with Alistair Barber.'

'All right, Tom.' I might think it was an emergency but Dad sounded as calm as ever. 'Take your time and tell me everything.'

I did my best, trying to put everything in the right order and not miss anything out. The quicker Dad knew exactly what had happened, the faster he could do something about rescuing Laura. I must have done pretty well because Dad hardly interrupted me at all. When I'd finished, he gave me a little pat on the shoulder to show how pleased he was with me.

'OK,' he said. 'You don't know how many men there are inside the house but you're pretty sure they're all in the tunnel.'

'They were,' I told him. 'Manson was going off to fetch them when I left. They were going to stop work and leave.'

'They'll have a lot of clearing up to do. Besides, they won't want to leave until it's really dark.'

'I hope not.'

'I'm sure of it. And I want you to know something, Tom. I'm very proud of what you've done this afternoon. You've been really brave.'

This was just about the first time anybody had ever called me brave. Coming from Dad, it made me sort of glow inside.

'I wasn't really,' I said. 'I was scared all the time.'

'That's what being brave is, Tom. Doing something even though you're frightened. Now I'm going to ask you to be brave for a bit longer.'

'I'll try.'

The way I was feeling then, I would have tackled Gerald Manson, the Druids and a whole army of ghosts.

'Good boy. Can you show me and my men the way down into the tunnel?'

'That's easy, only I'll have to borrow a torch. I broke mine on his head.' I was pointing at Sam.

'I saw you. I wasn't sure whether I was watching my son or Action Man.' Dad was smiling at me.

'I didn't half hurt my head on his belt buckle.'

'You'll recover. Besides, I think you hurt his stomach a lot more.'

'What's going to happen to him? Is he coming inside the house with us?'

'No. He's straight off to jail.'

'In that case, I think you'd better go through his pockets first. He's got the key to the room where Laura and Ali are locked up.'

'I'll do that now. You stay here. I shan't be long.'

Dad went off to talk to some of the other policemen, leaving me on my own. I didn't mind. I was still trying to get used to the idea that I might be brave.

'This is as far as we go, Tom.'

I'd led the police through the house and into the cellar. The wine-rack door was open, just as I'd left it.

'Aren't you going into the tunnel?' I asked.

'Not likely. Us police inspectors don't get mixed up in the rough stuff.'

I tried to look as though I believed him. All the same, I knew that if I hadn't been there, Dad would have been with the rest of the policemen. He'd only stayed behind to look after me. We stood and watched the men file into the tunnel. There were a lot of them, twenty of them at least, and several of them seemed rather nervous. I hoped none of them were hurt.

'You still haven't told me what you're doing here,' I said, once the last of the policemen had vanished into the tunnel.

'I haven't, have I? I suppose it's because of the door.'

'The door?'

I didn't understand what Dad was talking about.

'Didn't you notice how surprised I was when the door opened so easily this morning? I could see the lock had been oiled, and that's what started me thinking.'

'There must have been something more. You wouldn't have come here with all those men just because a lock had been oiled.'

'That's true. There was quite a lot more. For a start, there was what you and Laura had told me about the light you'd seen. Neither of you are the type to imagine things. Then there was Alistair's disappearance. Put those together with the oiled lock and there was obviously something pretty strange going on up here.'

'So Laura and me gave you the clue.' This made me feel almost as good as being told I was brave.

'You did indeed,' Dad agreed. 'Mind you, I already had the most important clue myself, only I was too stupid to see it. Do you remember me mentioning those criminals who were supposed to have moved into the Wroxford area, the payroll gang?'

'Yes. They were the reason you were taken off the search for Ali.'

'That's right. Well, it wasn't until I left here with you this morning that I realized something which had been staring me in the face for most of the week. There were all these weird happenings at a place called the Manson house and, surprise, surprise, the leader of the gang I'm looking for is called Alfred Manson. It was just too much of a coincidence, and I don't know how I missed it before. Anyway, that was more than enough to make me give up my Saturday afternoon in front of the television. I went back to the station to do some checking.'

'What did you check, Dad?'

It was like some adventure story in a book. I mean, I couldn't wait to find out what had happened.

'I started off with the name,' Dad told me. 'Manson isn't all that common and, sure enough, Alfred was related to the Wroxford Mansons. That meant that he'd know all about this house and I was pretty sure he must be up here. The only problem was, I couldn't think why. At least, I couldn't until I went back to the estate agent's. I had Mr Pettigrew hunt out the plans of the house. As soon as I saw them it was obvious what was happening.'

Dad stopped there, as though he'd explained everything, but he'd lost me again. Being brave didn't mean I had to be clever as well.

'It isn't obvious to me, Dad.'

'Well, that was when I learned about the tunnel. Originally it was supposed to go all the way from the house to the paper mill. Although it was never completely finished, it nearly was. There were only a few more metres to go when Wilberforce Manson gave up. And, by another strange coincidence, the paper mill is exactly the kind of business which would interest Manson's gang. The wages there are still paid in cash, so once a week there's a large amount of money kept in the factory safe. It wasn't very hard to put two and two together.'

'Let me guess,' I said happily, remembering what I'd heard Manson say. 'The money is in the safe on a Thursday night.'

Perhaps I wasn't that dim after all.

'That's right,' Dad told me. 'The workers are paid on a Friday.'

I'd have liked to talk some more about the Manson

gang but just then there was a shout from the tunnel. Although it sounded a long way away, I looked anxiously across at Dad.

'Do you think everything is all right?' I asked.

'There's no need to worry. Manson never has more than five or six people working with him. I've brought along plenty of men to handle them.'

'All the same,' I pointed out, 'they're taking an awfully long time to free Laura and Ali. The room they're in is only just down the tunnel.'

'My men will want to check the whole area is safe before they release them,' Dad said. 'It won't be long now.'

It wasn't, either. It couldn't have been more than a minute later that I saw four people hurrying along the tunnel towards us. At first I could only distinguish their outlines, two tall and two short. When they reached the nearest of the oil lamps, I could see their faces as well. It was Laura and Ali, together with two of the policemen.

Laura must have recognized us at the same moment because she suddenly started running. She made for Dad first, jumping up to give him a hug. Then she took me by surprise and turned on me. One instant I was standing there smirking at the fuss she was making of Dad. The next Laura had her arms wrapped around me tightly enough to crack my ribs. Worse still, she gave me a big, sloppy kiss before I could move my face out of the way. I mean, Laura might be my sister and I'm awfully fond of her, but I don't want her kissing me all the time, especially not in front of other people. It's embarrassing.

'Thank you, Tom,' she said. 'I knew I could rely on you.'

For one terrible second I thought she was going to kiss me again, but I managed to push her away before she'd made up her mind.

'Think nothing of it,' I told her. 'Stuff like this is all in a day's work for us superheroes.'

Laura laughed and I gave her a little punch on the arm to show how pleased I was to see her safe and sound, even if I didn't want her slobbering all over me. By this time Ali had joined us, and for once he was quiet. To tell the truth, he didn't look all that great. There were purple smudges under his eyes and he seemed decidedly peaky. Mind you, I'd probably have been a lot worse if I'd been locked up for as long as he had.

'Thank you, Tom,' he said, grabbing hold of my hand and shaking it. 'I really appreciate what you did.'

'It wasn't all me,' I mumbled. Ali was being nice and this made me almost as uncomfortable as being kissed. 'Laura did most of it.'

'I've already thanked her.'

Perhaps Ali wasn't that bad after all, I decided. Lock him up for four or five days and he became almost human.

'How are you feeling, young fellow?' Dad was asking. 'You've been through quite an ordeal, one way or another.'

'I'm a bit tired, sir, and very hungry.'

'I expect we can do something about both of those,' Dad said. 'I'll need a statement from you later but for the time being I think the most important thing is to get you back to your parents. You've no idea how they've been worrying about you. Sergeant Hargreaves, perhaps I can leave it to you to return the kids to their respective parents.'

The sergeant was one of the policemen who had released Laura and Ali. He started towards the steps leading out of the cellar, and they followed behind. After a moment's hesitation, I began moving in the same direction, but Dad dropped a hand on my shoulder to stop me.

'You might as well see it through to the bitter end, Tom,' he said. 'Provided you do exactly as you're told.'

It was a good moment, almost as good as when Dad had told me I was brave. In a roundabout kind of way, Dad was saying I wasn't a little kid any more. Laura had stopped at the foot of the steps and I was certain she was going to ask why she couldn't stay too. It must have been on the tip of her tongue but somehow she managed to hold it back. She just gave me a quick smile and started up the steps after the sergeant and Ali. There are times when I really do like her a tremendous lot. I mean, I know she's my sister, but she's still something special for a girl.

To be honest, Laura didn't miss a great deal. About a quarter of an hour after she'd gone, the main body of policemen came out of the tunnel. They had four prisoners with them, including Alfred Manson. Although this was the first really good look at him I'd had, I'd have known his name even if I'd met him in the street. When we'd been going up the stairs that morning, Dad had shone his torch on the pictures on the wall. They were all portraits of members of the Manson family, and they all had the same big, pointed noses and droopy eyelids. Alfred Manson looked just the same. I mentioned this to Dad, and he said the only person who would be doing a portrait of Alfred was a police photographer.

The most exciting part was going along the tunnel with Dad. It seemed to go on for ever, sloping downwards nearly all the way. Near the end, though, it levelled out and then started going upwards again. The very last part wasn't really a proper tunnel any more. This was where the Manson gang had been digging and there were no more bricks on the walls and ceiling, just pieces of wood stuck here and there to hold the roof up. It was much lower than the rest of the tunnel as well, and Dad had to bend down to avoid banging his head. Then it just ended in a blank wall of earth. There was a long piece of metal lying on the floor, which Dad picked up and stuck into the ceiling. It didn't go in very far before it struck something solid. Dad said this was the floor of the strongroom at the paper mill, and I was sure he was right. As far as I was concerned, we could have been almost anywhere.

When we eventually got back to the cellar, the prisoners and the rest of the policemen had gone. We found them outside, along with four police vans and a couple of cars. It didn't take long to load everybody aboard and, once the vans had gone, Dad was ready to leave too. It wasn't until my backside touched the car seat that I realized just how tired I was. My eyelids seemed to be made of lead and I was yawning so much I was in danger of dislocating my jaw.

'It's been quite a day, hasn't it?' Dad said, turning round from the front seat to speak to me.

'You can say that again.'

'It''s been quite a day, hasn't it?' he said.

'Oh shut up,' I told him, grinning in the darkness.

Dad may be a terrific policeman but he really does have a terrible sense of humour.

We are going down the drive by now and I twisted round in my seat for a last look at the Manson house. There wasn't much to see, apart from the dark outline of the house against the night sky. At least, there wasn't until I noticed the light flickering in the downstairs window and the shadow of the figure holding it. Before I knew it, I was wide awake and shivering all over. It took a real effort to remind myself I was the new Tom Venables, brave as a lion and afraid of nothing.

'Tell me something, Dad.' At least my voice wasn't squeaking. 'Are your men still searching the house?'

'No, we're leaving it until tomorrow. We'll bring up a generator and rig up some electric lights.'

'Have all the policemen left?'

'We were the last to leave,' Dad told me. 'What's the matter?'

'Nothing, Dad.'

I turned around in my seat for another look, but it was too late. The police car had rounded the bend in the drive and the house was no longer in sight. In any case, I'd probably been imagining things. Why on earth would the shadowy figure have had one hand raised as though it was waving goodbye to me? Or had it been beckoning me back? Suddenly I was shivering again and I didn't stop until we were halfway down the hill. Next year somebody else could make a fortune out of the conkers in the garden. Tom Venables, brave as a lion and afraid of nothing, had had enough of the Manson house to last him a lifetime.

Other great reads from **Red Fox**

Further Red Fox titles that you might enjoy reading are listed on the following pages. They are available in bookshops or they can be ordered directly from us.

   If you would like to order books, please send this form and the money due to:

ARROW BOOKS, BOOKSERVICE BY POST, PO BOX 29, DOUGLAS, ISLE OF MAN, BRITISH ISLES. Please enclose a cheque or postal order made out to Arrow Books Ltd for the amount due, plus 22p per book for postage and packing, both for orders within the UK and for overseas orders.

NAME _____

ADDRESS _____

_____

Please print clearly.

Whilst every effort is made to keep prices low, it is sometimes necessary to increase cover prices at short notice. If you are ordering books by post, to save delay it is advisable to phone to confirm the correct price. The number to ring is THE SALES DEPARTMENT 071 (if outside London) 973 9700.

Other great reads ✈ *from* **Red Fox**

THE SNIFF STORIES   Ian Whybrow

Things just keep happening to Ben Moore. It's dead hard avoiding disaster when you've got to keep your street cred with your mates *and* cope with a family of oddballs at the same time. There's his appalling 2½ year old sister, his scatty parents who are into healthy eating and animal rights and, worse than all of these, there's Sniff! If only Ben could just get on with his scientific experiments and his attempt at a world beating *Swampbeast* score . . . but there's no chance of that while chaos is just around the corner.

ISBN 0 09 9750406   £2.50

J.B. SUPERSLEUTH   Joan Davenport

James Bond is a small thirteen-year-old with spots and spectacles. But with a name like that, how can he help being a supersleuth?

It all started when James and 'Polly' (Paul) Perkins spotted a teacher's stolen car. After that, more and more mysteries needed solving. With the case of the Arabian prince, the Murdered Model, the Bonfire Night Murder and the Lost Umbrella, JB's reputation at Moorside Comprehensive soars.

But some of the cases aren't quite what they seem . . .

ISBN 0 09 9717808   £1.99

Other great reads from **Red Fox**

Adventure Stories from Enid Blyton

THE ADVENTUROUS FOUR

A trip in a Scottish fishing boat turns into the adventure of a lifetime for Mary and Jill, their brother Tom and their friend Andy, when they are wrecked off a deserted island and stumble across an amazing secret. A thrilling adventure for readers from eight to twelve.

ISBN 0 09 9477009   £2.50

THE ADVENTUROUS FOUR AGAIN

'I don't expect we'll have any adventures *this* time,' says Tom, as he and sisters Mary and Jill arrive for another holiday. But Tom couldn't be more mistaken, for when the children sail along the coast to explore the Cliff of Birds with Andy the fisher boy, they discover much more than they bargained for . . .

ISBN 0 09 9477106   £2.50

COME TO THE CIRCUS

When Fenella's Aunt Jane decides to get married and live in Canada, Fenella is rather upset. And when she finds out that she is to be packed off to live with her aunt and uncle at Mr Crack's circus, she is horrified. How will she ever feel at home there when she is so scared of animals?

ISBN 0 09 937590 7   £1.75

Other great reads from **Red Fox**

Discover the exciting and hilarious books of Hazel Townson!

THE MOVING STATUE

One windy day in the middle of his paper round, Jason Riddle is blown against the town's war memorial statue.

But the statue moves its foot! Can this be true?

ISBN 0 09 973370 6 £1.99

ONE GREEN BOTTLE

Tim Evans has invented a fantasic new board game called REDUNDO. But after he leaves it at his local toy shop it disappears! Could Mr Snyder, the wily toy shop owner have stolen the game to develop it for himself? Tim and his friend Doggo decide to take drastic action and with the help of a mysterious green bottle, plan a Reign of Terror.

ISBN 0 09 956810 1 £1.50

THE SPECKLED PANIC

When Kip buys Venger's Speckled Truthpaste instead of toothpaste, funny things start happening. But they get out of control when the headmaster eats some by mistake. What terrible truths will he tell the parents on speech day?

ISBN 0 09 935490 X £1.75

THE CHOKING PERIL

In this sequel to *The Speckled Panic*, Herbie, Kip and Arthur Venger the inventor attempt to reform Grumpton's litterbugs.

ISBN 0 09 950530 4 £1.25

Other great reads from **Red Fox**

Discover the exciting Lenny and Jake adventure series by Hazel Townson!

Lenny Hargreaves wants to be a magician some day, so he's always practising magic tricks. He takes this very seriously, but his friend Jake Allen tends to scoff because he knows the tricks will probably go wrong. All the same, Lenny usually manages to round off one of the exciting and amazing adventures that they keep getting involved in with a trick that solves the problem.

The books in the series are:

The Great Ice Cream Crime
ISBN 0 09 976000 2
£1.99

The Siege of Cobb Street School
ISBN 0 09 975980 2
£1.99

The Vanishing Gran
ISBN 0 09 935480 2
£1.50

Haunted Ivy
ISBN 09 941320 5
£1.99

The Crimson Crescent
ISBN 09 952110 5
£1.50

The Staggering Snowman
ISBN 0 9956820 9
£1.50

Fireworks Galore
ISBN 09 965540 3
£1.99

And the latest story—

Walnut Whirl
Lenny and Jake are being followed by a stranger. Is he a spy trying to recover the microfilm in the walnut shell Lenny has discovered in his pocket? The chase overtakes a school outing to an Elizabethan mansion and there are many hilarious adventures before the truth is finally revealed.

ISBN 0 09 973380 3   £1.99

Other great reads **from Red Fox**

The Maggie Series   Joan Lingard

MAGGIE 1: THE CLEARANCE

Sixteen-year-old Maggie McKinley's dreading the prospect of a whole summer with her granny in a remote Scottish glen. But the holiday begins to look more exciting when Maggie meets the Frasers. She soon becomes best friends with James and spends almost all her time with him. Which leads, indirectly, to a terrible accident . . .

ISBN 0 09 947730 0   £1.99

MAGGIE 2: THE RESETTLING

Maggie McKinley's family has been forced to move to a high rise flat and her mother is on the verge of a nervous breakdown. As her family begins to rely more heavily on her, Maggie finds less and less time for her schoolwork and her boyfriend James. The pressures mount and Maggie slowly realizes that she alone must control the direction of her life.

ISBN 0 09 949220 2   £1.99

MAGGIE 3: THE PILGRIMAGE

Maggie is now seventeen. Though a Glaswegian through and through, she is very much looking forward to a cycling holiday with her boyfriend James. But James begins to annoy Maggie and tensions mount. Then they meet two Canadian boys and Maggie finds she is strongly attracted to one of them.

ISBN 0 09 951190 8   £2.50

MAGGIE 4: THE REUNION

At eighteen, Maggie McKinley has been accepted for university and is preparing to face the world. On her first trip abroad, she flies to Canada to a summer au pair job and a reunion with Phil, the Canadian student she met the previous summer. But as usual in Maggie's life, events don't go quite as planned . . .

ISBN 0 09 951260 2   £2.50

Other great reads *from* **Red Fox**

THE WINTER VISITOR Joan Lingard

Strangers didn't come to Nick Murray's home town in winter.
And they didn't lodge at his house. But Ed Black had—and Nick
Murray didn't like it.

Why had Ed come? The small Scottish seaside resort was
bleak, cold and grey at that time of year. The answer, Nick
begins to suspect, lies with his mother—was there some past
connection between her and Ed?

ISBN 0 09 938590 2 £1.99

STRANGERS IN THE HOUSE Joan Lingard

Calum resents his mother remarrying. He doesn't want to move
to a flat in Edinburgh with a new father and a thirteen-year-old
stepsister. Stella, too, dreads the new marriage. Used to living
alone with her father she loathes the idea of sharing their small
flat.

Stella's and Calum's struggles to adapt to a new life, while
trying to cope with the problems of growing up are related with
great poignancy in a book which will be enjoyed by all older
readers.

ISBN 0 09 955020 2 £1.95

Other great reads **from Red Fox**

Fantasy fiction—the Song of the Lioness series

ALANNA—THE FIRST ADVENTURE
Tamora Pierce

Alanna has just one wish—to become a knight. Her twin brother, Thom, prefers magic and wants to be a great sorcerer. So they swop places and Alanna, dressed as a boy, sets off for the king's court. Becoming a knight is difficult—but Alanna is brave and determined to succeed. And her gift for magic is to prove essential to her survival . . .

ISBN 0 09 943560 8   £2.50

IN THE HAND OF THE GODDESS
Tamora Pierce

Alan of Trebond is the smallest but toughest of the squires at court. Only Prince Jonathan knows she is really a girl called Alanna.

As she prepares for her final training to become a knight, Alanna is troubled. Is she the only one to sense the evil in Duke Roger? Does no one realise what a threat his steely ambition poses?

Alanna must use every ounce of her warrior skills and her gift for magic if she is to survive her Ordeal of Knighthood—and outwit the dangerous sorcerer duke.

ISBN 0 09 955560 3   £2.50

The third title in the Song of the Lioness series, THE GIRL WHO RIDES LIKE A MAN will be published by Red Fox in May 1991.

Other great reads **from Red Fox**

The latest and funniest joke books are from Red Fox!

THE OZONE FRIENDLY JOKE BOOK
Kim Harris, Chris Langham, Robert Lee,
Richard Turner

What's green and highly dangerous?
How do you start a row between conservationists?
What's green and can't be rubbed out?

Green jokes for green people (non-greens will be pea-green when they see how hard you're laughing), bags and bags of them (biodegradable of course).

All the jokes in this book are printed on environmentally friendly paper and every copy you buy will help GREENPEACE save our planet.

* David Bellamy with a machine gun.
* Pour oil on troubled waters.
* The Indelible hulk.

ISBN 0 09 973190 8 £1.99

THE HAUNTED HOUSE JOKE BOOK
John Hegarty

There are skeletons in the scullery . . .
Beasties in the bath . . .
There are spooks in the sitting room
And jokes to make you laugh . . .

Search your home and see if we are right. Then come back, sit down and shudder to the hauntingly funny and eerily rib-rattling jokes in this book.

ISBN 0 09 9621509 £1.99

Other great reads from **Red Fox**

Two Enid Blyton books in one!

MR TWIDDLE STORIES

Mr Twiddle is a silly but lovable old man. He's always losing things—like his hat and his specs—he has trouble with a cat, gets bitten by a goose and, no matter how he tries, he just can't remember anything! This collection contains two complete books in one!

ISBN 0 09 965560 8   £1.99

MR PINKWHISTLE STORIES

Mr Pinkwhistle is small and round with pointed ears and bright green eyes. And he can do all sorts of magic . . . This collection gives you two complete books about Mr Pinkwhistle in one!

ISBN 0 09 954200 5   £1.99

MR MEDDLE STORIES

Mr Meddle is a naughty little pixie who simply *can't* mind his own business. He always tries to help others but by the time he's fed birdseed to the goldfish, sat in the butter, gone to bed in the wrong house and chased a policeman, people usually wish they'd never set eyes on him. This collection of stories gives you two complete books about Mr Meddle in one!

ISBN 0 09 965550 0   £1.99

Other great reads *from **Red Fox***

Discover the wide range of exciting activity books from Red Fox

THE PAINT AND PRINT FUN BOOK
Steve and Megumi Biddle

Would you like to make a glittering bird? A colourful tiger? A stained-glass window? Or an old treasure map? Well, all you need are ordinary materials like vegetables, tinfoil, paper doilies, even your own fingers to make all kinds of amazing things—without too much mess.

Follow Steve and Megumi's step-by-step instructions and clear diagrams and you can make all kinds of professional designs—to hang on your wall or give to your friends.

ISBN 0 09 9644606   £2.50

CRAZY KITES   Peter Eldin

This book is a terrific introduction to the art of flying kites. There are lots of easy-to-assemble, different kites to make, from the basic flat kite to the Chinese dragon and the book also gives you clear instructions on launching, flying and landing. Kite flying is fun. Help yourself to a soaring good time.

ISBN 0 09 964550 5   £2.50

Other great reads ✎*from* **Red Fox**

CRAZY PRESENTS Juliet Bawden

Would you like to make: Pebble paper weights? Green tomato chutney? Scented hand cream? Patchwork clowns? Leather ties?

By following the step-by-step instructions in this book you can make a huge variety of gifts—from rattles for the very young to footwarmers for the very old. Some cost a few pence, others a little more but all are extra special presents.

ISBN 0 09 967080 1 £2.50

CRAZY PAPER Eric Kenneway

Origami—the Japanese art of paper folding—is easy and fun to do. You can make boats that float, wriggling snakes, tumbling acrobats, jumping frogs and many more fantastic creatures.

There are easy to follow instructions and clear diagrams in this classic guide used by Japanese schoolchildren.

ISBN 0 09 951380 3 £1.95

Other great reads *from* **Red Fox**

AMAZING ORIGAMI FOR CHILDREN
Steve and Megumi Biddle

Origami is an exciting and easy way to make toys, decorations and all kinds of useful things from folded paper.

Use leftover gift paper to make a party hat and a fancy box. Or create a colourful lorry, a pretty rose and a zoo full of origami animals. There are over 50 fun projects in Amazing Origami.

Following Steve and Megumi's step-by-step instructions and clear drawings, you'll amaze your friends and family with your magical paper creations.

ISBN 0 09 9661802   £4.99

MAGICAL STRING   Steve and Megumi Biddle

With only a loop of string you can make all kinds of shapes, puzzles and games. Steve and Megumi Biddle provide all the instructions and diagrams that are needed to create their amazing string magic in another of their inventive and absorbing books.

ISBN 0 09 964470 3   £2.50